PUPPY LOVE

PUPPY LOVE

Larry Stewart

To order additional copies of this book, contact:
Xlibris Corporation
1-888-795-4274
www.Xlibris.com
Orders@Xlibris.com
133360

1

ALONE IN HIS bedroom on a winter night in 1960, clad only in jockey shorts, Sean O'Malley lay sprawled across the foot of the bed with his head dangling over the mattress. He was hashing over whether to join a street gang. Half his brain was telling him to be a black-shoe and join The Rebel Rousers, a brutal gang. The other half told him to be a white-shoe, find a sexy bobby-soxer, play sports, be popular, and be the high school hero.

A *Life* magazine and a boxy, black phone rested on the shag carpet in front of him, its thick extension cord snaking across the room. Mrs. Ferguson had been hogging the party-line for the past thirty minutes, preventing him from calling his best friend, Arnie Gallaway. Sean's parents refused to splurge for a private telephone line, so they shared the line with two other families. The deep, resonant voice of Wolfman Jack boomed from the bedside radio. When Little Richard began belting out *Lucille*, he rolled over and cranked up the volume.

Sean's bedroom looked like that of any fifteen year old high school sophomore. A musty smell from a pile of dirty clothes permeated the air. Ripping a picture of Grace Kelly out of the magazine, he hopped off the bed and tacked it between the pin-ups of Natalie Wood and Audrey Hepburn above a dresser that was overrun with model airplanes, bombers and toy soldiers. He tore out another picture of James Dean and tucked it in the mirror frame above an autographed, black and white glossy photograph of Marlon Brando.

Moby Dick, White Fang and a horde of other adventure books lay scattered around his room. Sean plopped back onto the bed and pulled out a *Playboy* from a stash of girlie magazines that he kept hidden underneath the mattress. He flipped the pages to the centerfold. After lusting at the photograph of Marilyn Monroe for a few minutes, he slid it under a fluffy pillow and picked up the telephone. Mrs. Ferguson was finally off and he quickly dialed Arnie's number.

"Hey, Arnie," he said, "have you heard about the rumble that's going to take place at."

"Shut off the darn music, numbskull," shouted Arnie, cutting Sean off. "I couldn't hear a word you said."

Sean belched, lowered the volume on the radio, rolled onto his side, pressed the phone against his ear and said in a low voice, "You heard about the rumble that's going to happen this Friday night at Orange Park?"

"No," said Arnie. "Who's duking it out?"

Sean wiped the sandy brown hair from his hazel eyes and said, "The Hell's Demons and the Night Riders of the Black Scourge."

"Holy cow," Arnie's voice blared, "those hoods would butcher their own grandmothers. The Slaughter brothers just joined the Demons. Those gangs are ruthless. You'd be nuts going anywhere near that park."

Sean sat up and pulled his knees to his chest. "I've got it covered, pal," he said. "Remember that old tree-fort up in the huge oak tree near the bleachers?"

"Yeah," said Arnie, "what about it?"

"It's so thick with branches and overgrown mistletoe and moss, nobody will see us. That place is completely hidden. It's the perfect hideout."

"Count me out Daddy-O," said Arnie, "I'll stick to frolicking with chicks."

Sean rolled off the bed and squatted with his back leaning against the wall. "Man, are you made out of chicken liver?"

"Are you calling me a coward?" Arnie gruffly said.

Sean grinned. "Ain't no one gonna to know we're hiding up there," he said. "It'll be like watching a flick, only in 3D. Come on, Arnie, it'll be a gas."

Several minutes later, Arnie slowly began to come around to Sean's idea. "Man, if we get busted by those punks," he said, "we're dog meat."

"Don't sweat it," said Sean, "we won't. It's a cinch. Whaddaya say?"

"I must be crazy for letting you talk me into this. Aw, heck, count me in. How 'bout Sal, does he know?"

"Yeah, he called me an hour ago and told me about it," said Sean, hearing a loud thump against his door. "Someone just knocked on my door. I gotta go. See ya at school tomorrow."

Excited, Sean hung up the phone and quickly stashed the *Playboy* magazine under the mattress. "Who is it?" Sean shouted at the door as he jumped up from the bed. Not hearing a reply, he opened the door and looked down the hall. Not seeing anyone, he shut the door began his exercise routine, flexing his muscles in front of the dresser mirror as he did most every night.

An hour later, after a hundred repetitions of sit up's, push-ups, deep-knee bends, squats and torso stretches, Sean studied his reflection in the mirror. He felt good about his physique, weighing 170 pounds and being nearly six feet tall.

*   *   *

At a quarter past eleven the coming Friday night, Sean slipped the straps of a pair of binoculars around his neck and quietly clambered out of his bedroom window. Lowering himself down the rope, he hopped onto the patio, hunched down and tiptoed to his three-speed Schwinn bicycle. He was careful not to trip as he pushed it along the side of the house below the window where his mother stood painting a canvas on an easel. He paused and listened to the syncopated music coming from the rumpus room window where his dad and his beatnik musician buddies were playing jazz. Sean was certain it was his dad blowing into the reed of a Sax.

Out in the tree-lined street, his head buzzing with excited anticipation, Sean mounted his bike and peddled down Arroyo Drive. Racing across El Camino toward downtown South San Francisco, he was spooked by the sound of screeching tires behind him. Rattled and dreading being rammed in the rear, his bike squiggled.

"Hey, asshole, get a horse," a voice yelled.

Regaining control of the bicycle, Sean saw Scott Simpson, sitting in the back seat of a convertible with two other kids. They were all laughing and Sean raised his arm and flipped them the bird, cussing at them as the car roared off.

Heading toward Papa Joe's pizza joint, Sean hopped the curb, popped a wheelie and threw his bike into a 360°, sliding sideways to where Arnie Gallaway and Sal Martinez were standing by their bicycles, with binoculars hanging from their necks.

"Smooth move, X-Lax," said Arnie, grinning at Sean.

"Man, some jerk nearly creamed me a few minutes ago," said Sean. "That bozo, Scott Simpson and his two cronies were in the backseat laughing their butts off. I'm gonna kick that guy's ass on Monday."

Arnie, tall, lean and wiry, scratched his sideburns and said, "That might not be easy, he's a boxer with lightning fast hands."

Sean laughed. "I ain't going to fight that punk with gloves in a ring. I'm talking bare knuckles."

Sal swiped his greasy black hair away from his dark eyes and said, "So, Daddy-O, are you ready for this brawl?"

"Been looking forward to it all week," said Sean. "I'm pumped. This is going to be like having a front row seat, watching *The Wild One.*"

"*Rebel Without a Cause,*" said Arnie.

"Yeah," said Sal, "*Westside Story* without music. This is the real thing. Let's get going, we don't wanna miss the action."

At a quarter to midnight, the three teens arrived at Orange Park. Their blood pulsing, they stashed their bikes in thick shrubbery and climbed up the wooden cleats into the tree fort to await the rumble. Speaking in hushed voices, they knelt in front of the peepholes in the rotting planks.

"That lamppost bothers me," said Arnie. "It's shining right up here."

"Quit worrying," said Sean. "We're safe."

"No one's going to be looking up here," said Sal.

The three kids started getting antsy at half past midnight.

"Maybe it's not going down," said Sal.

Arnie shrugged. "They might have called a truce."

"Wait a minute," said Sean, "I think I hear something. Look, over there," he pointed at the east entrance of the parking lot. "Here they come. Hot ziggity zam, it's going to happen."

The three boys raised their binoculars and peered through the gnarly branches at the stream of dimmed parking lights coming from the chopped and lowered hot rods of the Night Riders of the Black Scourge, jiggling across the parking lot. From the west entrance, they watched the slow procession of the Hell's Demons, revving the engines of their sleek Harley-Davidson and Indian motorcycles. The showdown finally arrived.

The rival gangs shut off their motors. With their binoculars pressed tightly to their eyes, the three teens watched the Demons, the meanest bikers they had ever seen, dismount their hogs. The two gangs swaggered toward one another in opposing lines. Looking tough as hell, the girls hung back by the hot rods and motorcycles with their thumbs wedged in the small slots of their jean coin pockets.

"Isn't that Sharon Mitchell the Homecoming Queen?" Arnie said.

"Yeah," said Sal. "Man, that chick's changed drastically since the last time I saw her. She's become one tough looking cookie."

Sean wagged his head. "You ain't kidding. Some of those icy faced floozies have tattoos. Hey," he said, pointing his finger at a blond girl. "I know that babe with the red jacket standing next to the black Harley. It's Kathy Svenson. She's in my history class. I can't believe she's with those raunchy broads. I've had a mad crush on her since I first saw her in junior high school."

Sal's brow furled. "Those biker chicks all look hot to me," he said. "I'd romp in the sack with any one of 'um."

Arnie and Sean looked quizzically at Sal before turning to watch the gangs, about 30 members each, trample and stomp toward each other. They were all garbed in tight-fitting dungarees, greasy white T-shirts, black boots, and black leather jackets, with their gang names emblazoned on the back.

One of the Demons, appearing to be the leader, had a scraggly black beard and wore a motorcycle cap slanted over his unruly mop of raven hair. Chewing fiendishly, he took off his jacket, flung it on the ground, ripped off his T-shirt and began puffing out his hairy chest. With a deadly grin, he flexed his muscles and grabbed a motorcycle chain from a fellow street fighter, and began slapping it hard against his palm without flinching.

"That crazy looking monster looks just like Bluto," said Arnie.

"Yeah, Bluto the Terrible," said Sal.

Sean wagged his head. "That creepy dude looks dangerous."

A Night Rider brandishing a baseball bat, and looking to be the leader of the gang strutted forth to meet his enemy. His hands glinted from the reflecting headlights as if he was wearing brass knuckles.

"Check out the jagged scar running down the side of that gorilla's face," said Sean. "Man, that's nasty."

"I've seen him at Bud's pool hall," said Sal. "They call him Scarman."

Their eyes glaring, the two gang leaders stood snarling at each other, from three feet apart. The gang members, armed with switchblades, clubs, chains and other lethal weapons, waited for the battle cry. One of the Demon bikers, a scraggly redheaded goon with a stringy goatee was wielding a tomahawk.

As the two leaders taunted one another, Scarman drew an imaginary line with his bat as if to mark the boundary of his turf, and appeared to dare Bluto to cross it. Bluto, his eyes crazed and twitching wildly, said something to Scarman and abruptly spit in his face. At that instant, the two gangs charged head-on in a thundering clash.

Bluto lashed out with his chain. Scarman ducked and swung his bat at Bluto's knees. Bluto went down like a sack of stones.

Sean squirmed as bones crunched and bodies began dropping. He shuddered when Scarman clobbered another victim on the side of his face. Bluto struggled back to his feet and charged Scarman, shoving a knife into his back. Scarman crumpled to the pavement. With a wicked look of vengeance, Bluto pumped his boot into Scarman's ribs. Bluto turned and was chain whipped on the back of his head by an enraged Demon.

With blood squirting everywhere and bodies scattering like bowling pins, Sean couldn't control his nausea and retched. Wiping the spittle, he looked at Sal and was shocked that Sal appeared to be enjoying the warfare.

Feeling nauseous, Sean looked at Sal with a disgusted expression and said, "Having a good time, Sal?"

"Bug off, twerp," said Sal, grinning.

"For cripes sake, Sal," said Sean. "What the hell's come over you?"

Sal squinted. "Are you some kind of pansy-ass?"

Sean flipped Sal the bird. "Drop dead wimp."

His olive complexion milky white, Arnie muttered, "It's a darn bloodbath."

"You've got that right," Sean grumbled. "It's so gory, my bloods curdling and my hands are all clammy."

Sal stared defiantly at Arnie and Sean. "You two sissies wet your pants?"

Arnie and Sean told Sal to bug off and shut his mouth.

Sean didn't want to be thought of as a pussy and forced his binoculars back to the peephole. At that moment, the tomahawk-wielding maniac swung his weapon and grazed a guy's scalp. Sean and Arnie cringed.

The gang fight was peaking and had shifted closer to the oak tree when Sal started hollering as if he was having the time of his life. Arnie, doubled over and gagging, jumped up and barfed. Panting and reeling with nausea from the putrid stench of vomit, Sean tried to control from having another choking spasm. The plank Sean was leaning against snapped free and sailed down onto the battlefield, clipping the shoulder of the redheaded maniac. Jerking his head around, in a frantic rage, the maniac viciously glared up at the tree fort, pointed his tomahawk and charged.

"Holy shit," Sean yelled, "That madman's seen us!"

Arnie and Sean panicked.

"Quick, Sean," shouted Arnie. "Grab a board and clobber the first punk who tries to get in here."

Sean ripped off a plank and hollered at Sal, "Don't just sit there on your duff, do something. That maniac with the tomahawk saw us. This is life or death, ya little squirt."

Grinning as if he was watching a comedy, Sal looked over at Sean and Arnie. "That cat just got smashed on the back of his skull with a tire iron. No one's coming up here, relax."

A few moments later, the sound of distant sirens infiltrated the damp night air. Arnie and Sean sat petrified on their haunches staring at Sal. Sal, whooping it up, never budged from the peephole. Arnie and Sean continued to stare at their friend in puzzled silence. This was a side of Sal they had never seen.

Sean wiped the sweat from his face with his sleeve. "Whew," he said. "That's some bloodbath taking place down there."

"It's ghoulish," said Arnie. "If that psycho hadn't got clobbered, we'd be dead-meat."

"You're right, Arnie," said Sean. "We'd be goners for sure."

As the sound of the sirens grew louder, the two gangs began fleeing the battlefield, leaving their mangled comrades twitching spastically on the ground. Within minutes after the gangs had fled, half a dozen squad cars, with flashing red lights, filled the parking lot.

Scared stiff, Arnie and Sean sat staring at Sal in silence as several ambulances arrived and the paramedics began loading the mutilated bodies onto stretchers.

When the parking lot was empty a half hour later, the three kids climbed down from the tree fort. None of them spoke a word until they were halfway home. Out of breath and gasping, they stopped peddling and laid their bikes down on the sidewalk.

"Holy smoke," said Sean, raising his arms. "My hands are shaking like crazy. That was sickening. I'm feeling queasy."

Trembling, Arnie said, "Me too. That was a frigging massacre."

Turning his attention to Sal, Sean said, "Hey, Sal, what's with the name calling, ya little pint-sized runt?"

"Yeah," said Arnie, "and the nasty looks?"

Sal shrugged and said, "So I liked it. I thought it was cool."

"Cool!" Sean shouted. "Are you loco. That was a damn slaughter."

"Just because you two are pansies, doesn't mean I have to be a wimp."

Arnie's wily blue eyes turned hostile and he raised his fists. "You calling me a pansy?"

Sean stepped between them. "Come on you guys, enough bloodshed. Wise up."

"Hey, I'm sorry, Arnie," said Sal. "I've never seen a real gang fight before. So, maybe I did get carried away. I don't know what triggered me to enjoy it so much."

Sean laughed. "You looked possessed by the devil."

"Face it, Sal," said Arnie. "You're way too scrawny to be in a gang. Those brutes would stomp your skinny butt."

Sal shook his head and grimaced. "Those dudes play for keeps," he said. "You think any of those guys they carted off were dead?"

"Naw," Arnie replied. "They'd have covered the bodies with white sheets."

Sal looked at Sean. "Are you still going to join up with The Rebel Rousers?"

"After witnessing that gruesome demolition," said Sean, "I'll stick to tussling with chicks."

"Now you're talking," said Arnie. "Besides, the good looking babes don't go out with punks."

Sean wiped the puke from his chin with his jacket sleeve. "Those raunchy broads sounded like cheerleaders rooting at a football game."

"Their nothing but floozies," said Arnie. "They grossed me out. Who the hell would want to make-out with a sleazy biker chick?"

"Just thugs, ruffians, hoods and punks," said Sean.

"As for me," said Arnie, "I say the hell with violence. I'm hanging out where the babes are fresh and wholesome."

Taking a deep breath, Sean said, "I'll second that motion. I want a chick that smells like fresh flowers and has smooth silky legs and a nice butt."

"And firm boobies," said Sal.

Sean shook his head. "I still can't get over Kathy Svenson being there. She doesn't fit the type."

"It surprised me too," said Arnie. "She's one of the most popular chicks in school and a pompom girl to boot."

"Yeah," said Sean. "And she's brainy too. I don't get it."

"Maybe it's just a passing phase," said Sal.

After chewing the fat for a few minutes, the three kids split up and headed home. Sean's hands remained shaky as he sneaked through the window, careful not to make the slightest peep. The little hand on the alarm clock on top of the nightstand was pointing at three o'clock when Sean crawled into bed.

2

A SHROUD OF mushy, gray fog engulfed the sky on the late Saturday morning Sean was meandering through Aquatic Park Marina in San Francisco. The marina was the base headquarters of the Sea Scouts where he was a member, and a place he frequented whenever he needed to clear his mind. He had spent the morning sailing on the San Francisco Bay aboard the *Silver Cloud*, a converted Boston whaler and was going to meet his father for lunch. They were going to have a pep talk about the birds and the bees.

Kathy Svenson began appearing frequently in Sean's nocturnal dreams since the night he saw her at the gang fight two weeks ago. She was always bubbly, shaking pompoms; performing jumping jacks, back flips, somersaults, and cartwheels on the sidelines of the high school football field in his dreams. But the images of her he had dreamt during the two previous nights proved to be nightmares. In his dream the night before, he asked her to go out on a date and she laughed in his face, jolting him wide awake in a stupor.

Sean was devising a plan that would catapult him into popularity and gain Kathy's favor when he stooped and picked up a flattened pebble. He aimed at a bobbing buoy and hurled it like a fast ball, skipping it over the small breakers and bouncing it off the buoy. Kathy was so popular, Sean was pretty sure she would mock and ridicule him if he ever gathered the backbone to ask her out on a date.

Tired of brooding over Kathy, he finally managed to blank her from his mind. When the fog lifted, he stared up at the majestic Golden Gate Bridge as he walked along the sand, mulling over whether to quit the

Sea Scouts. It was mostly because of the dorky square hat and goofy flair bottomed dungarees he was wearing that made him want to drop out. Every time he put on the dumb uniform, Sean hoped he wouldn't be seen by any of his classmates, especially Kathy. Having to wear that stupid outfit was the only reason he was thinking of saying goodbye to the Sea Scouts. He loved whiffing the salty sea air, feeling the cold wind against his face, and winning regattas.

He sat on the sand, watching some fellow Sea Scouts swab their sailboat, *Lightning Bolt* that Sean's crew had beat in a race to Point Reyes the weekend before. Listening to the haunting, baleful blare of a foghorn, he shut his eyes and began daydreaming about Kathy. He regretted having pulled her hair during their freshman year in his foolish attempts to gain her attention. When he opened his eyes a few moments later, the crewmates of *Lightning Bolt* were raising the fluttering main sail, the jib, the mizzen, and were shoving off in a flurry of activity. Standing up, he put his hands inside his pockets, slouched forward and ambled toward the pier.

Slightly rueful about his decision to break off from the Sea Scouts, Sean watched the rainbow spinnaker fill taut after *Lightning Bolt* had sailed out of the harbor. The sailboat cut sharply through the cresting swells, heaving and dancing like a prima ballerina. He looked out at Alcatraz, scuffed his heels, and walked toward a drinking fountain, thinking how he would miss his sailing buddies and the competition.

His thirst quenched by the cool water, he sat on a bench and brought a package of spearmint gum from out of his navy blue pea coat. As he began chewing, the shriveled and florid faces of two elderly women sitting at a table across from him caught his attention. The women, swaddled in tattered overcoats, were happily feeding breadcrumbs to a swooping flock of greedy pigeons and seagulls. The women waved at him and Sean politely smiled in return.

Waving goodbye to the two ladies, he left to meet his dad, who was fishing with his pal, Lou Marino. Most everyone along the wharf called Lou, Dago Lou, because of his throaty Italian accent. But not Sean, he thought it was disrespectful.

Walking lazily past the cable car turn-a-round on Hyde Street, he smiled when he heard the musical clanging of brass bells coming from a cable car, rumbling up the hill. When he arrived at Fishermen's Wharf, Sean whiffed the scent of crab coming from the boiling in pots at the outdoor fish markets. He was looking forward to having a fatherly chat and excited about seeing Lou, a scraggly-haired, crusty old fisherman and a very talented jazz musician.

Seeing his father and Lou, waving for him to come aboard the *Ana Maria,* a trawler Lou had named after his mother, Sean beamed. Lou was sitting on an upside-down tin bucket mending fishing nets with Snappy, a yellow parrot, perched on his shoulder when Sean stepped onboard. Lou was wearing his usual sandals, dirty khaki shorts, unbuttoned blue shirt, and a faded wool seaman's cap. His father had on his favorite Tam o' Shanter and wore a light windbreaker that was embroidered with green four leaf clovers.

"Grab a fishing pole son, and join us," said Sean's father, Marty after a hearty embrace.

"Too boring, Dad, I'd rather whittle."

"Aye, matey," said Lou in a gravely voice as he and Sean exchanged hugs. "You've been a stranger. Where've you been hiding?"

"School," replied Sean, "homework, and now girls. They've got me baffled."

"Beautiful day to be sailing," said Marty.

"Yeah, it was great," said Sean. "It's also one of the reasons I want to talk to you, Dad. I'm thinking about chucking the Sea Scouts."

"What?" Marty said with a surprised expression. "Don't be foolish. You love sailing."

Feeling a little sheepish, Sean said, "I know, but the uniform sucks big time, Dad. And chicks don't think it's cool."

Lou grabbed a wooden crate and smacked it with his hand. "Take a seat, matey," he said, handing it to Sean. "Your uniform looks fine."

"Thanks, Lou. But girls are always making funny faces when they see me wearing it. It really bugs me."

"You're just overreacting, said Lou, picking up a small pine stick and handing it to Sean. "Here, chip away on this."

"Thanks," said Sean, sitting on a crate beside his father and taking out his Swiss Army pocketknife.

"You've been sailing since junior high school," said Marty. "You need to do what you love. There are plenty of woman who love the sea and would be proud of your uniform."

"Your dad's right," said Lou as he started building a fire for the barbecue. "I was about your age when I took to the high seas. I didn't pay much mind to women. I had fallen in love with the sea. Not that I wasn't attracted to dames. I've had my fair share with some mighty fine gals, who loved the sailing outfits I wore."

As Lou and Sean's father commenced to lecture on establishing priorities and the birds and the bees, Sean's eyes shifted from the parrot to Lou's sunken chest. Faintly visible beneath a mat of kinky gray hair was a faded tattoo of a bucking galleon in a sea of swirling froth. Both of Lou's arms were covered with tattoos of anchors, mermaids and sea dragons and other nautical lore. With the parrot resting on his shoulder and his ruddy, weather-battered face, Lou looked like he had just stepped off the gangplank of a pirate ship.

"You've been sailing as long as I've known you," said Lou.

"Yeah," said Sean as he shaved off a sliver from the stick, "but now girls have me going batty. There's this one girl who is driving me absolutely nuts."

Marty popped open a can of beer and said, "You going to quit snow skiing too, son?"

"No way, Dad, I'd never stop downhill racing. I love it too much. Besides, girls love that kind of daring, bravado stuff."

"I would rather be wearing Bermuda shorts when I go to school to teach," said Marty. "But I'm okay with wearing a coat and tie. Or even a suit on occasion."

"Your father's right," said Lou. "Why do you care what other people think about how you're dressed?"

"It's the way girls look at me when they see me wearing this goofy outfit."

"You need a lesson on establishing priorities, son," said Marty. "Youth is short-lived. You're a handsome lad. Girls will soon be crawling all over you. There are plenty of women who love the sea. But the choice is yours. Do what you want. You're in control of your life."

"I'm listening, Dad."

"Do you consider yourself an individual?" Marty asked.

"I sure do."

Marty wiped his thin mustache. "You can't be an individual if you go along with the crowd or care about what immature young girls think. Do you think the seamen in the Navy consider their uniforms dumb?"

"I, uh, I guess not."

"They're mighty proud," said Lou.

"And prouder yet when their dress whites are filled with ribbons and stripes, and gold and silver medals," said Marty.

"Thanks, Dad, and you too, Lou, you're right. I love the sea too much to give up sailing. Besides, I helped build that sleek boat."

Lou's parrot, Snappy squawked, "Scoundrel, scalawag" as Lou tossed a couple chunks of abalone on the grill. Sean smiled when Lou's one-legged, beady-eyed monkey, Hurdy Gurdy, hopped topside and sat on the hatch cover. He was scratching his armpits, making funny faces and sniffing as Sean sat conversing with his father about the birds and the bees. Lou reached into a cooler, pulled out a banana and handed it to Sean. Sean tossed it at Hurdy Gurdy.

"I have one other problem," Sean blurted as Hurdy Gurdy peeled the banana and wolfed it down. "I can't muster the courage to ask this one particular girl out. "I really like her a lot. But it would kill me if she said no."

"It doesn't take courage, son," said Marty. "It takes self-confidence. It gets easier each time. The longer you wait, the harder it gets. You'll never know until you ask her."

"But I hate rejection, Dad. It would kill me if she said no."

"No one likes being rebuffed," said Marty. "Find out what her interests are. See if you share a common ground. Maybe she likes to ski, dance, or play volleyball."

"She can ice skate," said Sean excitedly. "I've seen her at the skating rink and man she's good, I mean she's great." Brian turned gloomy. "But I don't know how to ice skate."

"It's as easy as skiing," said Marty. "It's all about balance, coordination, and concentration. And you're adept at those."

"Ask her if she'd be willing to teach you," said Lou as he flipped over the abalone.

"And let her watch me make a fool of myself."

"Take a lesson or two on your mother and me," said Marty.

"Thanks, Dad. That's so cool."

The three sat talking about the birds and the bees while eating abalone, and shucking shrimp and crab.

After a couple hours of Marty and Lou's tutoring Sean in the art of breaking the ice with girls, Marty looked up at the position of the sun, "You had best be going home, son," he said, setting down his fishing pole and standing up. "You know how your mother gets when you're late."

"Oh, yeah, I know," replied Sean.

Holding Sean's shoulders, Marty said, "It's been a pleasure talking to you today. Let's do this more often. I spoke with the principle at your school the other day. He told me that you're doing exceptionally well and may get a scholarship."

Sean's eyes lit up. "You're kidding me," he said.

"No, it's the truth. I want you to know that your mother and I are very proud of you, son. Keep up the good work."

"Thanks, Dad. You and Lou have taught me a lot today about girls." Sean handed Lou the mermaid he had carved during their conversation. "A little something for the bowsprit," he said. "I'll finish it the next time I visit."

The three hugged and Sean left to catch the bus home.

He got off at the bus stop and walked to where he had left his bicycle chained to a light pole. Turning the tumbler to release the lock, he decided that instead of going home, he'd drop by Arnie's pad. A brilliant plan had come to him on the bus ride, an idea that would clinch their quest to be the coolest, most popular kids in school. He pedaled a half mile to Arnie's house and leaned his bicycle against the side wall next to Sal's bike, and jogged down the steps into the bomb shelter that Arnie's dad, Chuck, had converted into a den. Sal and Arnie were shooting a game of eight-ball in the smoke filled room and Frankie Lyman was singing *I'm not a Juvenile Delinquent* coming from a portable radio.

"I got us a dynamite plan," said Sean, plopping sideways onto an old chesterfield and resting his feet on the armrest. "This one's gonna work. Every chick in school will be hot to trot with us."

Arnie took a drag from a cigarette and smirked. "Is this another one of your dimwit ideas?"

"This one's sure-fire, I guarantee it."

"Like your hair-brain scheme to heist Wyatt Earp's tombstone," said Sal.

Arnie laughed. "That blasted thing must have weighed a ton."

Sean scratched his nose. "How the heck was I to know that thing was so darn heavy?"

"Common sense," said Sal. "Every kleptomaniac around here would want to snatch that trophy. Wyatt Earp was a legend."

"Yeah, well, you guys went along with it," said Sean.

Arnie chalked his cue stick. "So what's this new scheme you've concocted?"

Sean was in the middle of laying out his plan when he mentioned Judge Tommason's name, and his buddies hooted derisively.

"You've flipped your lid," Arnie howled. "Rip off Judge Tommason's hub caps. You've got to be joking."

"Arnie's right," said Sal. "That judge is bad news. If anybody got caught stealing his hubcaps, that tyrant would send the guy to the joint. I heard that old fart sentenced some poor kid to life in prison for knocking-up his daughter."

"We won't get busted," said Sean. "That judge's notoriety is why we'll be the most popular kids in school."

Sean finished explaining his plan.

"Sean might be onto something," Arnie said, lining up a shot, "I'm starting to dig it."

Sal balked. "I'd go along, but I'd better not," he said. "Getting busted for driving without a license and being on probation, I'd be in deep water if we got nabbed and I had to stand in front that old geezer. But I double dare you guys. Heck, I triple dare you."

Sean looked at Arnie. "What about you, are you in?"

Arnie wiggled his chin and stuck out his hand. "I like it.

The two shook hands and Sean said, "We just need a getaway car."

"My neighbor down the street, Sandy Cliffhouse might be game," said Arnie.

"Yeah, Sandy," said Sean, "he's cool."

"And a darn good keyboardist," said Sal. "That cat can bang on those keys."

"Sandy's always talking about how he's gung-ho for some hair-raising antic," said Arnie, sinking the eight ball. "We're getting together tomorrow for a jam session. I'll ask him."

"I think Sandy will go for it, Arnie," said Sean, "because he's always telling me how he's up for pulling off something risky."

"He tells me the same thing," said Arnie.

Sean racked the balls, chalked his stick and said. "I've been thinking about Kathy Svenson all day. If we pull off this caper, I'm pretty sure she'll go out with me."

Arnie smacked the cue ball and laughed. "Wild side or not, no way that stuck-up chick will go out with you. She's way too conceited."

"Yeah," said Sal, "she thinks her poop doesn't stink. Maybe you should lower your expectations. Besides, ain't she going out with that low-life boxer, Scott what's-his-face?"

Sinking the fifteen ball into the side pocket, Sean said, "Scott Simpson, that ego-maniac, she ain't going out with that creep. Besides, I'm going to kick his butt on Monday."

"You've been saying that for almost a month and nothing ever happens," said Arnie.

"His time's coming," said Sean, looking at the clock on the wall. "Holy cow, I've better get home. See you alligators later."

In a tizzy over being late for dinner, Sean pedaled as fast as he could while drumming up an alibi. Turning the corner onto his block, he spotted a sleek, black 1955 Thunderbird parked in front of his house. It was gleaming under a haloing streetlight. He stopped alongside the small car and lowered the kickstand. *Hot ziggity zam, a '55 T-Bird. This is cool, real cool. I wonder who it belongs to.* With admiring eyes, he slowly circled the car and peered through a round window.

"Hands off, ya little runt," Devin Daniels called out as he strolled down the pathway from Sean's house to the sidewalk. "Look but don't touch. I don't want your cooties smudging the shine. Just rubbed her out and polished her this morning."

Devin was the preppy boyfriend of Sean's older sister, Heather, a senior in high school. Devin lived across the Bay in a frat house on the UC Berkeley campus where he studied law. As always, he was sharply dressed in Ivy League clothing. His gold-rimmed glasses, short cropped reddish hair and greenish-blue eyes, gave him a scholarly presence. He was also a track and field jock and marathoner. Devin's boasting about his family reeking of wealth, irritated Sean.

Sean swiped the hair from his eyes. "Holy mackerel, golly, is this your car?"

Devin winked at Sean and said, "Got her last week. Hell of a good deal. I couldn't pass her up. This baby's going to be a classic someday."

"Gees, she's snazzy, Devin. This is some hot set of wheels. She sure does shine. Sean walked to the front of the car. "Smooth lines, I bet this buffed beauty hauls butt. What'll she do?"

"Had her pushing 120 coming across the Bay Bridge on the way here," said Devin, wiping his glasses with his Cal Blazer. "Taking your

sister on a spin down to the Santa Cruz Boardwalk tomorrow, think I'll
open her up and let her rip. Give your Heather a thrill."

Sean nodded. "Gee willikers, this thing flies."

Devin put his glasses back on and folded his arms over his chest. "If
she doesn't," he said, "I'll throw a pair of wings on her."

Poking her head from out of her second floor bedroom window,
Sean's older sister, Heather shouted, "Hey, pipsqueak, you'd better get
your fanny inside. Mother's furious. I'll be down in a jiffy, Devin," she
said in a softer voice.

"Best you get inside like your sister told you, kiddo," said Devin. "You
know how your Mom gets when you're late."

"Yeah, I know. Why do you and my sister keep referring to me as
being a midget? I'm almost six feet tall."

Devin sized Sean up. "It does appear you've had a sudden spurt of
growth. Guess its force of habit."

In less than a minute, Sean heard the taps from Heather's spiked, high
heel shoes as she came prancing down the walkway. He could smell her
perfume as she glided past him and took Devin's arm. "Sorry I took so
long," she said.

Sean wasn't wearing blinders. He had watched his sister transform
from a frumpy, chubby girl into a full-blown woman. Heather was amply
stacked and had long, shapely legs. But Sean knew she had rules, strict
rules. Heather went to Mercy High School, a Catholic girls' school, sang
in the church choir, and attended Mass faithfully every Sunday. She even
went to Bible school twice a week. Other than smooching, Sean was sure
his sister didn't allow much else. The way she prayed and acted so saintly,
she didn't need to go to confession. Sean was positive touchy-feely and
hanky-panky were definite no-no's. The give-away was the tiny crucifix
around her neck. Sean had never seen her not wearing it.

Heather was wearing a pink shawl, furry beige sweater over a scarlet
blouse and had on and a frilly knee-length skirt over half a dozen
petticoats.

"My," said Devin, "you certainly look lovely tonight."

Heather's blue eyes beamed. "Thank you. You're sweet." She pecked
him on the cheek and then waggled her fingers at Sean. "As for you,
kiddo, mother's fuming. You're in deep trouble."

"Back off, beauty queen," said Sean, sniffing her neck. "That stuff
stinks, makes me sick. And knock off the kiddo crap."

Heather rounded her pink lips. "Drop dead, buster. Look, I'm not fooling, mother is boiling mad. Why didn't you at least call and tell her you'd be late? You know how she gets."

"I tried, but you were yakking on the phone like always. Just like you hog the bathroom every night, taking bubble baths, then come gliding out all slathered in goop and acting like Miss Teenage America."

"What about you, dunce," Heather fired back, "posing in front of the mirror like your Hercules. You could at least lift the toilet seat when you tinkle."

"Hey, you two," said Devin. "Knock it off."

Sean looked at Devin. "She thinks she's so cool because she's a hot-shot volleyball player."

"So what if I'm proud that my team's in first place," said Heather. "At least I excel in something. You can't even get up the courage to ask a girl out."

"That's enough out of you two," said Devin. "Let's go or we'll be late for the movie."

"In a while, crocodile," said Sean. "I'd best get the big bang over with."

Sean wheeled his bike past the wrought iron gate into the side yard. Through the window he could see his two younger brothers, Trevor and Kevin, kneeling in front of the black and white television console, watching Laurel and Hardy and munching popcorn in the living room. His mother, Rachel, was sitting on a stool at the counter sipping tea when Sean merrily walked into the kitchen through the side door. She set the cup onto a saucer and glared at Sean as Squeaky, a big yellow and black dotted Myna bird squawked "Cracker" from within a round cage.

"Hi, Mom," said Sean. "Sorry I'm so late. I got wrapped up studying for a big history test on Monday at Arnie's pad and lost track of time. Then I had a flat tire on the way home and had to take it off and patch it."

"Don't embarrass me with another one of your cockamamie excuses," Rachel shouted. "You had me worried sick."

"I tried calling, Mom," said Sean, picking up a cookie and feeing it to Squeaky, "but the line was busy. Heather's always hogging the phone."

Rachel's olive complexioned face was puffy and red with anger. "Wipe that smirk off your cocky face," she said. "I'm fed up with you taking me for a fool. Until you learn to abide by these simple rules and regain my respect, you're grounded."

"Ahh, Mom. It's the truth. Honest."

"It doesn't matter, Sean. I've warned you a thousand times that it's your responsibility to be home on time for dinner." Rachel got up and walked to the doorway of her art studio. "Your dinner is in the oven, and don't forget to do your chores. We need eggs and cottage cheese from the milkman."

"Yes, Mom, but golly . . ."

"And don't forget to put out the trash."

"Yes, Mom, but gee whiz, it wasn't my fault the darn tire blew out. Can't you have some sympathy? Shucks, it won't happen again. I promise."

"Don't give me another empty promise," said Rachel. "Case closed." She disappeared into her studio.

Sean served himself a plate of steamy tamales, poured a glass of milk and went into the dining room. Sitting at the table, he began mumbling about the cruel and unjust punishment as he ate. After washing the dishes and straightening up, Sean went to the doorway of his mother's atelier.

"Is Dad downstairs in the music room?"

Rachel dabbed the canvas with a paint brush. "Your Father's out with his bohemian friends, playing music."

"The tamales were delicious, Mom."

"Don't flatter me in hopes of changing my mind. By the way, some of the neighbors have been complaining about the noisy ruckus coming from that go-cart contraption, whizzing up and down the street early in the morning on the weekends. Put a muffler on it, or junk it."

Sniveling, Sean shrugged and said, "I will, Mom."

"And take down those disgusting, filthy pictures in your bedroom."

"Yes Mom."

3

SANDY CLIFFHOUSE JUMPED out of the chair later in the day when Arnie told him about Sean's idea to rip off judge Tommason's hubcaps. Arnie and Sandy were pretty tight friends and Sandy, a junior at South City High School, eagerly agreed to drive the getaway car. That night, Sean set his alarm for six the next morning.

The fog was so dense in the morning when Sean poked his head out of the window that could barely see the house next door that was only ten-feet away. Charged up, he called Arnie and quickly showered, dressed and ate the light breakfast his mother had prepared before he dashed out of the house.

At seven sharp, Sandy shut off the engine of his raked '55 Ford and coasted into the parking lot behind the courthouse. Shortly later, the three kids watched the judge drive in and park his black Buick in its usual spot.

"You guys sure you two want to go through with this?" Sandy asked Arnie and Sean after the judge had walked into the courthouse. "You two might end up shackled in chains and busting rocks on some prison farm, convicts."

Snickering, Arnie held up a large flathead screwdriver and said, "This is just minor mischief. Besides, the fog's way too pea-soupy for anyone to see us."

A few minutes later, Arnie and Sean were crouched behind a low-wall surrounding the parking lot, peering through the moist fog at the judge's car.

Squinting and grinning wildly, they were scanning the courthouse windows when Sean, spinning a tire-iron in his hands, whispered, "This is it, the perfect crime. We're about to become celebrities, maybe even legends."

"Let's hustle before the fog burns off," said Arnie in a commanding voice. "I'll take the two on the left. You take the two on the right. Whatever you do, don't drop them."

Sean looked at Arnie cross-eyed and said, "Bug off, dipstick, I ain't no bumbling twit."

"Okay, numb-nuts," said Arnie, "but make it fast and let's pull off this caper of the century."

The two brazen kids quickly leapt over the wall, hunched forward and scurried across the parking lot. In under a minute, they popped off the judge's hubcaps, tucked them under their arms and darted back to Sandy's car. As Sandy was pulling away, the 3 kids stared at the judge's black rims and howled in laughter. When Sandy shifted into third gear, the kids were feeling high as a kite on a windy day.

*   *   *

Sal tapped Sean on the back during English class and said, "You mind if I take some of the credit for heisting the judge's hub caps?"

"Heck no," said Sean. "Sure, Sal, welcome aboard."

Throughout the day, the four kids bragged about their daring heist. After school, a large milling crowd of disbelievers followed the kids to Sandy's car in the South City High School parking lot.

"You guys don't believe us," shouted Sean at the large crowd of students, "just wait. You'll see."

Sandy unlocked the trunk and the four kids, floating in seventh heaven, reached inside and pulled out the hubcaps. Adrenaline surging through their bodies, the boys hoisted the hubcaps over their heads, gloating as if they had won the coveted Wimbledon Cup.

The large pack of kids started jeering that they didn't believe the hubcaps were the judge's."

"Follow us and see for yourselves," shouted Sandy.

"That judge's car is naked as a jaybird," hollered Arnie.

Half the student body piled into cars and formed a cavalcade on the drive to the courthouse. A lot of hooting and hollering erupted when the stream of cars rolled past the judge's black-rimmed Buick.

That night, inside his bedroom, Sean proudly hung his trophy on the wall next to a picture of Grace Kelly. Arriving at school the next morning, Sean, Arnie, Sal and Sandy were campus celebrities, strutting around all day with big smirks, slapping hands and bragging. Kathy Svenson even flirted with Sean for the first time, wiggling her hips and winking at him.

The elevated mood Sean was feeling abruptly ended when he got home after school and saw a police car in front of his house. Overcome with an extreme case of the jitters, he turned his bike around and raced down the street to Arnie's pad. Arnie and Sal were gulping soft drinks when Sean charged into the kitchen and began ranting about the police car he had seen in front of his house.

"Yeah, I know," said Arnie. "The cops were here too."

"Aw, crap!" Sean shouted. "How'd anybody find out? Nobody saw us. We pulled that off scot-free."

"The fuzz can't pin anything on me," said Sal, "I wasn't even there."

"What are you talking about," said Sean. "Everyone in school thinks you were in on it."

"Man," moaned Sal, "if we get busted, I'm in deep water."

"Quit bellyaching, Sal," said Arnie, we ain't been caught yet. We'll figure something out."

"Some jealous stoolie musta ratted on you guys," said Sal.

Sean slammed his fist on the pool table. "I betcha anything it was that Scott Simpson. Man I'm gonna stomp that snitch's butt. What did the police say?"

"You think I'm crazy," said Arnie. "No way did I answer the door."

"Aw heck," said Sean. "We need to come up with an alibi."

"I didn't swipe the dang things," said Sal, "but one of those hub caps is hanging in my bedroom. We'd best give them back."

"Give um back," said Sean.

"We have to," said Arnie. "Sal's right, it's the best thing to do, and the sooner the better. The next time you want a crime partner, find yourself another patsy."

"Hey, goodie two-shoes," said Sean, "you accepted the dare."

"It was your idea, numbskull," said Arnie. "Let's cut the bad mouthing and come up with a plan."

Sean rubbed his chin in thought. "Okay, I agree with you guys," he said. "Let's turn 'um in to the police station and tell the cops that someone's trying to frame us."

"How'd we get them?" Arnie asked.

"We found them dumped on our front lawns. Whoever stole the darn things wants us to take the blame. We're just returning the hub caps like law abiding citizens."

"Clever," said Arnie, "it's so simple, it might work. That is if you can maintain your composure. You're pretty shaky."

"Look who's talking," Sean told Arnie before he turned toward Sal. "You'd best get home and bring that hubcap over here. Let's meet in an hour."

"Why should I go," said Sal, "I didn't steal them?"

"Just go get that dang hub cap," said Arnie. "Sean and I will take care of the rest."

The police car was gone when Sean arrived back at his house. Climbing through his bedroom window, he hoped like crazy that the hubcap was still hanging on the wall. He sighed when he saw it and tiptoed across the room and stuffed it into a burlap sack.

A little over an hour later, Arnie and Sean walked into the South San Francisco police station and Arnie plopped the burlap sack on the counter.

"What's in the bag?" The police officer asked.

"Hub caps," said Arnie.

"Someone's trying to pin a rap on us," said Sean.

"I found two of them on my front porch yesterday when I got home from school," said Arnie.

"Me too," said Sean. "It was all the kids were talking about today at school that we stole judge Tommason's hubcaps. Some rat fink is trying to set us up."

The police officer carefully scrutinized the two boys. "Do you know who this person is?"

"No," said Sean, "but I have a strong suspicion it's a guy who has it out for me."

"What's his name?"

"It's just a wild guess," said Sean. "I don't have any conclusive proof."

The officer looked at Arnie and said, "What about you?"

"I'm in the same boat," said Arnie, there are some kids out to get me too."

The two boys were laughing up a storm over their brilliant performances at the police station when they got back to Arnie's pad.

"That cop swallowed it hook, line and sinker," said Sean as they began shooting a game of nine-ball.

"I'm sure glad that mess is out of the way," said Arnie.

"Yeah, me too," said Sean. "That was a close call. Let's talk about something else."

"Hey, hunting season's just around the corner. Why don't you come along?"

"Really," said Sean excitedly. "Heck, I've wanted to go ever since you first told me about those hunting trips with your dad and his buddies. The reason I couldn't go last year is because I was grounded."

"You're always getting grounded."

"Guess I'll have to be a good boy for a while. Be neat to get a feel for the old west like it was back in the days of Daniel Boone and Davy Crocket. Heck, I'd love to go. Where are you going hunting?"

"Up in the high Sierras," said Arnie. "There are plenty of big bucks, mule deer and whitetail roaming in those mountains. Maybe poach a rabbit or two."

"I'll skip the poaching part," said Sean, chalking his cue tip. "One close encounter with the law is enough for me. But I'd love to go hunting with you. At least it's legal. What about Sal?"

"He's coming," said Arnie, "He almost bagged a nice buck last year, but came down with a case of itchy fingers."

Sean laughed. "I remember."

"You need to get a hunting license pronto."

"Are they expensive?"

"Naw, they're cheap."

"Where do I get one?"

"Department of Fish and Game," said Arnie. "I'll give you the rundown later. Your old man got a rifle?"

"Naw, my dad's not into killing animals. He fishes but throws them back. What's a rifle cost?"

"My dad's got a bunch," said Arnie, lining up a shot. "In fact, he just bought a new rifle. You can use his old lever action 30.06 carbine and one of his .38 caliber revolvers. The rifle's got a ten-power scope. You'll need to clean it up and oil it."

"I've never done that before," said Sean.

"I'll show you later. It's easy."

"Are you sure your dad won't mind?"

"Heck no," said Arnie, "he likes you. So does my mom. They think you're a good influence on me."

"My parents say the same thing about you," said Sean. "Tell your dad that I'll polish his rifle and pistol till they sparkle like new."

"Sal and I are going to Coyote Point Rifle Range this Saturday to get in some target practice. Why don't you come along with us?"

"Sure," said Sean. "This sounds like a kick in the butt."

"You just need a couple boxes of ammo," said Arnie, sinking the nine ball, "you can afford that, can't cha?"

"Nice shot. Yeah, I got some money stashed from caddying. And I get paid from my newspaper route tomorrow."

*   *   *

A week before the hunting party was to set out for the Sierra's, Sean sat between Arnie and Sal at the Coyote Point Rifle Range. They were leaning with their backs against a low stone wall and their legs stretched out in front of them. The afternoon sunshine dappled prisms of colorful light against their closed eyes as they inhaled and exhaled with their arms folded over their chests. After ten minutes of meditation and enjoying the warm breeze, they opened their eyes.

"Thanks for the venison, Arnie," said Sean. "That was tasty."

"Told you so," said Arnie. "And that meat was frozen from last year. Wait until you taste the fresh stuff."

"Great recipe," said Sean. "My mom soaked it in red wine overnight. And last night she rolled it in flour and fried it in bacon grease, like your mom told me. Everyone loved it. Even my sister raved and she rarely eats meat. I sure have been feeling anxious about this hunting trip and bagging a deer. That is, if I do."

"You will," said Sal.

"What about the buck you missed last year," said Sean, "what happened?"

"I told you," said Sal. "I had him in the crosshairs, but my hands started shaking and I missed him. But I think I grazed his ear."

"Sal's trigger happy," said Arnie. "That's why we're here doing these breathing exercises. It helps to calm you down. Any luck with that Kathy babe?"

"I wish," said Sean. "She's been driving me loony lately. As hard as I try, I can't bring myself to ask her out. I get tongue-twisted. Even with all the razzing I get from you guys, and everyone else, I still can't get up the courage."

"Practice with your sister," said Sal. "That's what I did."

"I tried," said Sean, "but she breaks out laughing and I wind up feeling like a bungling klutz."

"Try rehearsing in front of the mirror," said Arnie.

"That's easy," said Sean. "It's the face-to-face stuff that makes me choke. I can't even muster the guts to strike up casual conversation with any girl. I totally freeze."

Arnie brought his knees up to his chin and stared at Sean. "You seem to be of average intelligence. Nice build, no body fat, somewhat good-looking. Why not compare hunting girls to hunting does. You know what the difference is, don't ya?"

"Sure, the rifle."

"Good," said Arnie. "What else?"

Sean scratched his scalp. "I don't know. What?"

"Ammo, for one thing and cunning, cleverness and practice helps," said Arnie. "Now let's zero in on that bull's-eye and hone our skills."

The three got up and walked to the rifle range.

"Anyone can slay a doe," said Sean while they were loading their rifles. "But you can't capture a doe. Even if you did, you could never tame it. The doe's home is the wilderness, not a cage."

"Who's talking about a cage, knucklehead," said Arnie. "I'm talking about the things pretty chicks like. You know, fragrant flowers, chocolate bonbons, fudge brownies or anything sweet. Girls go ape over that sort of stuff. It's all ammo."

"And poems," said Sal. "Girls love poems. Write Kathy a poem."

"What if I did all that and she still laughed at me."

"Geez, you're a lunkhead," said Sal. "I know what your problem is. It's rejection. That's your nemesis."

"You're right," said Sean, "that and that fink Scott Simpson. They're my arch enemies."

When the kids ran out of ammunition an hour later, they drew back their last targets.

Smiling proudly, Sean looked at his bullet-ridden target, scattered with holes surrounding the bulls-eye. He glanced at Sal's target. Two holes were smack-dab in the bulls-eye. Sean looked at Arnie's target. There was nothing left of the bull's-eye. It was torn to shreds.

"Not as good as yours, deadeye," Sean told Arnie. "But mine's not too shabby."

"Not bad for a couple of rookies," said Arnie. "You guys are catching on fast. Get those scopes zeroed in and you'll be sharpshooters."

"When'd you start hunting, Arnie?" Sean asked.

"I was a tenderfoot twelve when I nailed my first buck, a four-point mullie. I'll never forget my dad handing me his bowie knife and telling me to gut it."

Sean grimaced. "You had to gut it?"

"Yeah," said Arnie. "After I sliced open the deer's belly, my dad told me to stick my hand inside and pull out a sack. Man, it was grizzly. It was so slimy and warm, my whole body broke-out in goose bumps."

"Gees, I'll bet," said Sal.

"But the second time was like cutting a piece of cake."

*   *   *

When hunting season rolled around, Sean's ten-power scope was zeroed in. The sky was black on the early morning the hunting party set out in three trucks with camper shells on opening day. Arnie's dad, Chuck was a rugged hulk of a man. He hailed from Texas and spoke with a country twang. Chuck was accompanied by two of his good friends, Chet Peek and Lloyd Perkins. Both were raised in Virginia and spoke with southern drawls. Wearing boots and western hats, the three men looked like gun toting cowboys.

A light dusting of fresh snow covered the low foothills. Higher up in the Sierra Mountains, the three trucks stopped and the hunting party spread out on foot. After an hour scouring the area for hoof tracks, they met up again at the trucks.

"We gotta go higher," said Chet, adjusting his holster. "The big bucks ain't comin' down to forage unless they have to."

"You're right, Chet," said Chuck.

"There ain't nearly enough snow pack to force the big critters down to feed," said Lloyd.

"That's for dang sure," said Chuck. "We'd best get our tails up to a higher elevation if we want trophy racks."

They got back into the trucks and traversed up the steep terrain. It was well past night fall when they stopped at nine thousand feet. With the light from 4 lanterns, the three boys pitched the tents and gathered rocks to form a fire ring. Finished, the kids grabbed flashlights and went into the forest to gather kindling and firewood.

When the campfire was crackling, shooting flames and sparks into the dark, star-studded sky, the boys leaned against boulders and raptly listened to Chuck and his two mountain-men buddies spin yarns from former hunting exploits as thick juicy steaks were broiling on a grill above the fire.

After they finished eating, the three men filled their tin cups with Jack Daniels and began swigging as they continued to recant their tales in the wilderness while the kids roasted s'mores, sipped soda pops from straws and listened intently.

The temperature was below freezing when everyone crawled into their tents and slipped into long johns. Inside his sleeping bag lying between Arnie and Sal, with his head resting on a pillow, Sean wondered how it would feel to take an animal's life, and would he be capable of pulling the trigger. Listening to the sounds of hooting owls, the rustling wind, and other night creatures, Sean finally fell asleep.

Two hours before dawn, Arnie shined his flashlight on Sal and Sean's faces and tapped them on their shoulders. "Time to get crackin' boys," he said. "Sal, you fetch some more logs for the fire and brew a pot of cowboy coffee."

Groggy eyed, Sal sat up and mumbled, "Yeah, yeah."

"Sean, you can help me whip-up breakfast. The coolers are in the back of my dad's truck," said Arnie. "The red ones have the food. The blue ones have the pots and pans and other cooking stuff."

Sean stretched his arms, yawned and rubbed his eyes. "Sure, but I've got to take a dump first. Brrr, it's friggin' freezing."

"Grab a spade," said Arnie. "Dig a hole and bury the crap when you're finished. And watch out for poison oak. It's all over the woods. You know what it looks like, don't you?"

"For gosh sake, Arnie," said Sean, "would you back off. Of course I know what the stuff looks like. This ain't the first time I've camped in the outdoors. I've been camping since the Cub Scouts." Sean looked at Sal and sniffed. "Hey, Godzilla breath, you smell like dog pooh."

"Yeah, Sal," snorted Arnie. "Do everyone a favor and brush your teeth."

"And gargle too," said Sean.

"Would you two get off my case?" Sal spouted.

"Anyone told you that you snore and talk in your sleep, Sal," Arnie said.

"Yeah," grumbled Sal. "But it beats sleepwalking. I had a friend who walked in his sleep. One night he fell down the stairs and almost broke his neck. Poor kid was in agonizing pain for a couple months."

"Yee gads, that gives me the creeps," said Sean.

An hour later, the hunting party hungrily finished wolfing down platters of scrambled eggs, bacon, sausage and spuds. As the old-timers sat formulating a plan, the kids packed lunches and stuffed their thick down jacket pockets with snacks and soft drinks. Their rifles loaded with the safeties on, bandoleers of bullets crisscrossed over their chests, and holsters strapped around their waists, the boys climbed into Chuck's truck. The three trucks split up. Chet drove up a logging trail along the north ridge and Lloyd headed up a south ridge fire trail. Chuck and the boys dropped down into a canyon, zigzagging, and cutting through trees.

Chuck stopped his truck and said, "You boys get out here. We'll be working the ridges, driving 'um down to you. Don't squeeze the trigger until ya gottem in the crosshairs."

Nodding excitedly, the kids got out of the truck and Chuck drove off quietly. It was moonless and pitch-black, yet Arnie stalked off as if he could see. Sal and Sean flicked on their flashlights and followed behind Arnie.

Arnie turned and grumbled in a low voice, "Turn those dang lights off, and cut out the blabbing. The deer can hear you clumsy jackasses for miles. Let's not spook um."

"Hey, Arnie," said Sean, "just because you're some kind of full-blooded Indian brave with uncanny eagle eyesight doesn't mean I can see in the dark."

"Yeah, Arnie, I ain't even a half-breed," said Sal in a gruff tone. "I can't see a darn thing. I can't even hear you walking with those moccasins, not snapping a twig or crackling a dry leaf."

"You should be a ballerina," said Sean, shining his flashlight on Arnie's face.

Appearing disgusted, Arnie strode off in the dark as if he knew where he was going.

Sal and Sean kept their flashlights on and whispered.

"You ever kill an animal?" Sal asked Sean.

"Nope, except for flies, insects and other bugs," he replied. "I've caught fish, but my dad always makes me toss them back in. How 'bout you?"

"Naw, but I came close last year," said Sal. "I had that buck in the crosshairs and then my hands started shaking like a jigsaw. You think you can?"

"I'm not sure, but I guess I'm gonna find out. That is, if we even see any deer."

The sun was just starting to rise when the roar of gunfire began echoing over the mountains and across the canyon. Arnie rested his rifle on a fallen log and pulled out an ivory handled six-shooter from his holster. He twirled the pistol a few times on his finger and slipped it back into the holster. In the near freezing air, Arnie took off his jacket and wool shirt, tied a white and blue handkerchief around his head, put on a coonskin cap and raised his binoculars to his eyes. Looking serious and sniffing the air like a hound dog, Arnie scanned the mountainside. His body lean and wiry with a predacious face and cleft chin, Sean thought Arnie to be the perfect specimen of a venery hunter.

"Aren't you frigging cold?" Sal asked Arnie.

"I'm used to it."

"Thanks for inviting me, Arnie," said Sean. "I like being in the wilderness."

Arnie cupped his ear with his hand and whispered, "Shush, their coming."

Sal's eyes were pressed against his binoculars when he asked Arnie, "What's coming?"

"My pop and Chet, and Lloyd," said Arnie, pointing. "Can't you see the deer the trucks are driving toward us?"

"I don't see anything," said Sean, looking through the scope of his rifle at the valley where Arnie was pointing.

"Neither do I," said Sal. "I think Arnie's got X-ray vision."

"You dodos are blind as bats. The whole hillside is full of deer. They're coming right at us. Over there, at the base of that bluff," Arnie pointed, "a harem of does and a couple of forked horns."

"Where?" Sal asked.

"In that covey of bull-pines," said Arnie.

"I see 'um," said Sean excitedly. "Man, I got a beefy four-pointer in the crosshairs." Sean cocked his rifle and slammed a bullet into the chamber. He raised the scope to his left eye and took off the safety.

"Don't be trigger happy," said Arnie, reaching over and lowering the barrel of Sean's rifle. "Be patient. Let 'um get closer."

As cold as it was, Sean began sweating and his entire body tingled. Dark shadows were darting in every direction in the thick woods as the deer moved closer to the base of the canyon. As if spooked, the herd of deer charged into a grassy meadow, heading straight to where the kids lay with their rifles resting on a large log.

The herd was fifty yards away when Arnie whispered, "Let 'um get closer."

When the sound of clopping hooves onto rocks filled the air, Arnie yelled, "Fire at will." Arnie raised up on his knees, and squeezed off a single round. Sean flinched, watching the four-point mule deer crumple to the ground in a loud thump.

Arnie looked at Sean and pointed. "What are you waiting for, that's a nice 3-pointer. Drop him."

His eye on the scope and the cross-hairs bouncing wildly, Sean was doing his best to ward of off the buck fever Arnie had warned him about. Unable to keep his hands from trembling, Sean pulled the trigger. He missed and cocked again and fired. The 3-pointer almost landed on top of them and Sean turned and brought the scope to his eye and kept firing round after round at the sprinting deer's backside. Sal and Sean stood up and continued firing until Sal nailed a buck in the hindquarter. The deer buckled and Sal put another bullet in the deer's butt and it dropped.

Holding the rifle over his head and jumping up and down, Sal shouted, "Did you see that? I did it. This is so neat."

Sal was still whooping and hollering when the three trucks pulled alongside of the kids.

"That was some mighty fine shooting, boys," said Chuck.

"Yesiree, you kids did mighty good," said Chet. "You should be proud of yourselves."

"It was a stampede," said Sean. "I can't believe I missed. That buck almost took my head off."

"Arnie had the best shot," said Sal. "He nailed that sucker in mid-air."

"Yeah," said Sean, "right smack between the eyes."

Chuckling, Arnie said, "I was going for the neck. Your buck's still twitching. Better get over there and put him out of his misery."

Sal's face twisted and he said, "Huh?"

With a big smirk on his face, Arnie said, "Ain't no porters here to do it for you. Then gut 'em. Ya don't want the meat to go rancid. Your buck ain't dead yet."

"You'd best show 'em how it's done, Arnie," said Lloyd.

"Then help 'em clean the deer," said Chuck. "You know the boy don't know how."

"All right, knucklehead," said Arnie. "Let's go zap your deer. Then I'll show ya how to gut him and butcher the meat."

After they got to Sal's deer, Arnie showed Sal where to aim. Sal, looking grim, took out his pistol fired a round into the deer's heart.

When the two deer were hanging from a tree branch, Arnie, showing no emotion, slit his deer's belly with his Bowie knife. Sean and Sal cringed when Arnie stuck his hand inside deer's sack and pulled out the steaming innards and gizzards and held them in front of Sal. "Now it's your turn, pal."

"Man, that's gruesome," said Sal, bending over and dropping to his knees. When he finished retching, Sal raised his head up and blurted, "I can't do that."

Sean managed not to throw up.

"Looks like you'd best do it, son," said Chuck, "don't think the boy has the stomach for it."

A few hours later, Arnie and Sal stuffed the wrapped meat packages into duffel bags filled with ice. They cleaned the deerskins and put them in another duffel bag.

Remaining nauseous and feeling down for having succumbed to buck fever, Sean asked Arnie, "What do you do with the carcasses?"

"Leave 'em for the grizzlies and mountain lions," said Arnie. "They'll be feastin' tonight." Arnie looked over at Sean. "Would you stop looking so darn dejected?"

"He was right in front of me and I choked," said Sean. "I don't get it. It's impossible that I missed."

Arnie placed his hand on Sean's shoulder. "The day's young, Sean. You'll have another crack."

After a night of listening to loud sounds of grunts, snorts and bellows, the next morning, they drove up, down and across mountainsides. The three trucks skidded to a halt and Chet jumped out and dropped a six-point mule deer from nearly three hundred yards. The rack had a spread of almost thirty inches. At dusk, Chuck nailed another trophy buck. Sean's spirit sank to an all time low from having missed two more easy opportunities.

Throughout the next day, Lloyd raised and lowered his rifle at least a dozen times. Each time he'd say the same thing, "Too small, not enough meat. I got a big family to feed."

At the crack of dawn the next day, Sean's eyes lit up when he spotted a large buck with a huge rack in the far distance. "Stop the truck!" Sean hollered as the three trucks screeched to a halt. Sean hoped out of the truck and ran to the edge of a sheer drop-off cliff with the scope held to his eye.

"Go head and take him, Sean," said Lloyd.

The cross-hairs bouncing like crazy all around the lone buck, nibbling on a bush of wild berries across the deep ravine, Sean said, "Naw, that's okay. I'd most likely miss the way my hands are shaking. You take him."

"That's enough food to last a year," said Lloyd as Sean released the safety, cocked and fired. The buck shuddered and took off like a rocket.

"Great shot, Sean," hollered Chuck, "you nailed him."

"But he's running like a bat out of hell," said Sean.

"He'll go down in a minute or two," said Arnie as they ran to the trucks. "We'll track that monster down."

It was almost noon when they found the six pointer. Sean sank down on a snow covered tree stump, rubbing his face and saying a silent prayer, and dreading to have to gut the deer.

"That was great shot, pal," said Sal.

"Yeah, buddy," said Arnie, "and so darn far. He must have been a quarter mile away."

"The way my hands were shaking," said Sean. "It's more like a miracle."

"My hands were shaking too," said Sal. "The butt's a lot bigger than the neck."

"Don't worry about gutting him," said Arnie, "I'll do it."

Just before sunset, the hunting party lay on the grass, staring intensely at a gorge. There was just enough light to see and the only sounds was their whispering and the rustling of branches and cackling of birds when they spotted a trophy buck and three does. The deer were moving slow and chewing on blueberry branches. Lloyd carefully set his binoculars down, raised the rifle and released the safety. He was about to place the scope to his eye when he saw the fangs of a coiled rattlesnake about to strike him between the eyes from three feet away. Jerking back in a state of panic, the rifle dropped from Lloyd's hands. Lloyd quickly covered his panic stricken face with his hands.

Arnie swiftly swatted and sliced the snake's head off with his Bowie knife.

"It's okay, Lloyd" said Arnie, dangling the headless snake in front of Lloyd, "it's dead. I killed it."

Terrified and trembling, Lloyd removed his hands from his face and watched Arnie hurl the snake's body in the brush. Lloyd quickly snatched his rifle and the hunters watched the buck's front legs buckle and listened to the echo of the gunshot as the buck crumpled to the ground.

"Man, that was a close call with that serpent," Sal told Lloyd after a round of back slapping congratulations and they hurried to the trucks. "You're one lucky guy. And that was one fantastic shot considering all."

Sean shook his head and said, "That was spooky. I thought you were dead for sure. Those fangs scared the life out of me."

"I guess I owe you my life, Arnie," said Lloyd, patting him on the back.

"I'll settle for a Coke."

"That's a deal," said Lloyd. "That was sure a ghastly sight. I've never been so frightened in my entire life. You're fast, Arnie. I'm surprised I managed to nail that buck."

"I guess that makes you a hero, Arnie," said Sean.

After a hearty breakfast the next morning, the hunting party headed back down the mountain. Sean was feeling jacked-up about bringing home the meat and not having had to do the gory gutting.

4

ETURNING HOME FROM the hunting trip, Sean wearily crawled into bed. The moment he closed his eyes, vivid images of Kathy Svenson began appearing in his dream. She was standing on a sandy beach dripping wet, wearing a grass skirt and a teeny bikini top. Water was spraying from her silky blond hair as she danced the hula in a blurring quiver. She slowed the tempo to a tantalizing tease, puckering her lips and curling her index fingers, beckoning for him to come to her. Kathy's face was so invitingly salacious, Sean was jarred awake with his arms stretching out to touch her. He nuzzled his head back on the pillow, closed his eyes and desperately tried to restart the dream.

In the morning, after a hot shower, he wiped the steam off the mirror and screamed, "Ah, heck. Not zits. Have mercy." He stared at the outbreak of pimples that had erupted on his face overnight and thought to himself, *Just when I'm on the verge of conquering my fears, this has to happen. Now she'll never go out with me.* He dashed down the hallway to his sister's bedroom and pleaded to her.

Fortunately, Heather, in a most un-sisterly like gesture of kindness, felt pity and tossed him a jar of Noxema from her glass top vanity.

"Put some on every night before you go to bed," said Heather, fluffing her hair in a huge pompadour that resembled a beehive. "In a week or two, it'll be cleared up. Now get out of my room. I need to get dressed."

"Thanks sis. You're not so bad after all."

"Have you asked that girl out yet?"

"I'm working on it."

"Give her that poem you wrote, it's very cute."

*   *   *

Luckily, Heather was right about his face clearing up. After a week of agony, the acne vanished and Sean began feeling a surge of self-confidence while he sat at his desk in history class determined to ask Kathy out on a date. As he had been doing since the day he hoisted the hubcap over his head in the school parking lot, he wrote her another poem. Every time he looked at Kathy, his mind became impaired, regretful for all his imbecilic behavior in trying to gain her attention in junior high. She was sitting two rows across from him with her nose pointed up, looking like a prude, and chewing pink bubble gum. He fell into a fantasy dreamscape, imagining his arm draped over her shoulders as they road lip-locked through the Tunnel of Love at Playland at the Beach.

It's now or never, dumbo. You either ask her out or your butt is going into the annals of cowards as the world's biggest yellowbelly, gutless buffoon ever born. Get off your duff and act like a man.

At the clang of the bell, Kathy bolted from her desk and joined the running of the bulls in the chaotic corridor. Sean stuffed the poem in his shirt pocket and quickly followed her, his eyes keenly locked on the backside of her pleated skirt. Her brusque voice rang-out in his head as he chased after her, thinking about what she would say after he asked her out. *Are you kidding me? Me go out with you? I wouldn't go out with you for a million dollars; you imbecile, you idiot.* When Kathy stopped at her locker, his eyes dropped to her tanned calves. *Wow, what legs, what a tush. She's one fine doll. Okay, dumbo, the time has come to ask this fine babe out.*

His hormonal juices rushing in a flood, Sean tapped Kathy on her shoulder. She turned and looked at him as if he was a bothersome pest. Staring into the blue eyes of the most divine creature on the planet, he froze. Lockjaw set in, and he began praying that she wouldn't ridicule him in front of everyone. His muscles tense, his legs twitching, and his hands moist, Sean felt on the verge of collapsing.

With a look of petulance, Kathy nonchalantly said, "Oh, hello, Sean. Is something wrong?" She waited impatiently for him to say something. "Why are you looking at me like that? What is it you want?"

"Ah, I was w-wondering if y-you'd like to, ah," Sean stuttered.

Looking at him oddly, she said, "Like to what? Don't just stand there. Look, Sean, I have to get to my next class. I don't have all day. Say something. Hey, are you the one who's been writing me all those poems?"

He swallowed and wondered if he should tell her. "Aw, yeah."

Her annoyed expression changed to a flirtatious smile. "I thought it might be you. They're really quite lovely and very clever, thank you. Now, what did you want to tell me?"

Trying his best to act casual, Sean blurted, "Would you like to go to the movies Friday night? I mean go out on a date?" He felt the urge to run.

Kathy beamed brightly. "Really, sure, what time?"

Stupefied by Kathy's receptive acceptance, the tension Sean felt eased slightly and he boldly said, "Well, the movie starts around 7:30, how 'bout I pick you up at 7?"

"7's cool," she said, her white teeth gleaming in the gloomy hall light. "I have to be home by eleven."

"That's okay."

She blew out a big pink bubble until it popped, sucked it back into her mouth and smiled. "What's playing?"

"Rebel Without a Cause."

Her eyes lit up. "I've heard it's a great flick," she said excitedly. "I've been dying to see it."

Knowing this might be the deal breaker, Sean said, "Oh, ah, I don't have a car."

"That's okay. I enjoy walking. It's good exercise. Or my dad can drive us."

Sean tweaked his lips. "I'd prefer to walk. I'm getting a car soon though. I have my permit. I'm going to take the drivers test on my birthday in October."

"Cool. What kind of car are you getting?"

Sean's knees stopped buckling and he said, "I don't know. I just know it's going to be a convertible."

"Groovy, I love ragtops." She took out a book and a binder from her locker, banged the metal door shut and twisted the tumbler. She turned to Sean with a perky smile. "Are you coming to the football game after school on Friday?"

"Sure, I always go," he said as the warning bell rang.

"Well, I'd better hurry or I'll be late for class," she said.

Still dumbfounded by Kathy's eagerness to go out with him, Sean smiled. "That's okay, I've gotta get a book. I'll see you at the game on Friday."

With a cute goo-goo eyed look and curling her pink-nailed fingers in a wave, Kathy said, "I'll give you my address in the cafeteria during lunch."

"Oh, that's okay, I know where you live."

She looked at him quizzically and said bye-bye and Sean's eyes followed her as she gleefully skipped down the hallway and turned the corner. He flipped up the button down collar of his new light blue, Ivy League shirt, feeling glad he had opted for the preppy look. Grinning like the cat that ate the canary, Sean coolly sauntered down the hallway into the boys' bathroom.

Scott Simpson and his two cronies were standing by the window, dragging on cigarettes and looking tough. Feeling high from Kathy's receptiveness, Sean only stared at them and slammed his fist into the paper towel dispenser. He could feel the temperature rising in his body as he stood at the urinal. *You've got to put an end to this. Not now. Not three against one. That rat-fink's time will come.* Finished washing and drying his hands, he coolly turned and strutted out the doorway.

After school let out, dreamy-eyed and feeling like he was walking on a cloud, Sean dropped by Arnie's pad to collect his winnings.

"Got me a date with Kathy Svenson," Sean boasted as Sal and Arnie were shooting a game of pool and chalking their sticks. "You guys need to pony up the 5 smackers we bet."

Arnie and Sal started laughing hysterically and reneged on the bet.

"Hey, you two, I won that bet fair and square," said Sean. "You guys owe me, so cough up."

"Get off it," said Sal. "Time's run out, pal. The statute of limitations has long expired."

"Yeah, Sean," said Arnie. "We made that bet eons ago."

Sean laughed. "All right, so it took me a while, but a bet's a bet."

Sean held his ground and the three argued for a few minutes before he let them off the hook.

"Man," said Sean, raising his hand to his neck, "I've had it up to here with that creep, Scott Simpson."

"You've been saying that for months," said Sal. "Talk's cheap, when are you going to do something?"

"Yeah, Sean," said Arnie. "Don't just talk about it, get into action."

"Soon," said Sean. "That punk's time has come. I'm going to kick his butt."

After a half dozen games of eight-ball, Sean walked home to do his homework while day-dreaming about his date with Kathy Friday night.

*   *   *

After watching Kathy jumping and swirling the pompoms during the junior varsity football game after school on Friday, Sean walked home on cloud 9. He went straight into the garage, changed into his gym clothes and began his routine of relentlessly smacking the punching bag, shadow boxing and skipping rope.

Finished working out and lathered in sweat, at five thirty sharp, Sean locked himself in the bathroom and stepped inside the shower. He vigorously scrubbed his entire body for twenty minutes with a scented soap, shampooed and crème rinsed his hair and turned off the water. After toweling himself dry, he wiped the steam off the mirror, smiled and splashed hot water on his cheeks. Patting shaving crème on his face and shaving his peach fuzz, he began singing "Taste your lips of wine anytime night or day. Only trouble is, ah gee whiz, I'm dreaming my life away."

"Will you hurry up?" Heather shouted, pounding on the door. "I need to get ready."

"Go take a flying leap," Sean fired back, and burst into a slightly off key version of "Be bop a loo la she's my baby."

Sean continued shaving and singing as Heather's tantrum escalated and she started jimmying the lock. When he finished shaving, he put on his jockey shorts, snapped the elastic band and slapped his flat stomach.

Ignoring the pounding, he studied his reflection in the mirror and was pleased that he was in top physical condition.

"Quit your bellyaching," he shouted. "My time has come."

He winked in the mirror and squeezed some white goop onto his palm, rubbing his hands together. Humming, "Brylcream, a little dab will do it," he ran his fingers through his hair and meticulously combed a ducktail behind his head. Paying no attention to his sister's ranting, he fluffed a big wave in front and patted his cheeks with English Leather. After striking a half-dozen poses for the final primping, he slipped on a terrycloth robe, and suavely opened the bathroom door.

Her face slathered in white cream and her hair loaded with curlers, Heather shoved him in the chest and hollered, "It's about time; you little squirt."

Sean wagged his head and said, "Geez, look at you with all that yucky goop on your face."

"It's a girl's thing, smart aleck," said Heather. "Mother told me you finally got up the nerve and asked that girl out. Congratulations." Heather leaned closer and sniffed his neck. "Ummmm, you certainly smell virile," she teased.

He smiled. "The tide's changed, sis, it's my turn. Got any tips on getting a kiss?"

"It's always the girl's call," she said, grinning. "She'll let you know if she wants you to kiss her. Don't come on too heavy. You might frighten her."

With a devilish grin, Sean said, "I'm thinking more along the lines of French kissing, a little fondling and the big you-know—what."

"Ye, gads, you're so uncouth."

Coming up the stairs, carrying a laundry basket, their mother, Rachel said, "Would you two stop bickering?"

"Sorry, Mom," said Sean, moving out of his mother's way. "But Heather started it."

"Look, Mother," Heather shrieked, pointing at the toilet. "Your pathetic son has done it again. There's yellow pee on the toilet seat."

"Good grief, Heather," Sean retorted. "What about the mess you make with all those bloody what-cha-ma-call-its."

"How dare you."

"Quit your squabbling," Rachel scolded, stopping at the doorway to the laundry room. "That is a disgusting and inexcusable habit Sean. Will you please raise the seat?"

"Yes Mom."

Heather stepped into the bathroom. "Scram, wise guy," she hollered and slammed the door.

Whistling *The Girl Can't Help It*, Sean went to his bedroom. After tying the shoelaces of his blue suede Hush Puppies shoes, he slipped on his new sports coat, and stood in front of the dresser mirror. He winked, creased his dimples and went downstairs for supper. Sean's two younger brothers, Trevor and Kevin were seated at the dining room table. After

Rachel recited grace and was serving a chicken casserole, Sean asked, "Where's Dad?"

"His jazz quartet is playing at The Sixteen Mile House. I'm taking your brothers after dinner."

"Aw, Mom," pleaded Trevor, "Flash Gordon's on tonight."

"Do we have to, Mom?" Kevin said. "All my favorite TV programs are on tonight."

"Your father is expecting us."

"It'll make dad feel good," said Sean, tossing the spinach salad.

"If it'll make dad feel so good, why aren't you going?" Kevin snipped.

"Yeah," said Trevor.

Sean gave his brothers a condescending look. "I've seen him play a thousand times. But tonight," he chimed, "I got me a date with the prettiest girl in the entire school."

"There's nothing more important than showing your father respect and moral support," said Rachel. "And you boys are to wear your new suits."

"Tell dad I'm sorry I can't be there," said Sean. "Oh, thanks for the new sport coat, Mom. It fits perfect."

"Can't have you going out on your first date wearing rags," said Rachel, suddenly staring at Sean. "Look at you! You're spilling salad dressing on your new jacket."

"Gosh darn it," Sean grumbled. "I'm sorry, Mom."

"Take that jacket off and put on a bib."

Sean washed the blue cheese salad dressing off his coat and put on an apron. After dinner, Trevor and Kevin scampered to their bedrooms to change as Sean straightened the table and washed and dried the dishes. When he finished, he took off the apron, slipped on his sport coat and went into his mother's studio.

"Sorry to interrupt, Mom," he said politely, studying her latest oil painting of his two brothers fishing from a riverbank.

Kneeling on a cushioned prie-dieu, clutching rosary beads, his mother said, "You're not."

"This is good, Mom, really good."

"Thank you."

"Can I borrow ten dollars? I'll pay you back. I have two caddy jobs this weekend."

"Is ten enough?"

"It's plenty, Mom."

"Fetch my purse. It's on the dresser in my bedroom."

He ran upstairs, grabbed her purse and came back.

Rachel opened the purse and took out her wallet. "Are you sure ten is enough?"

"I won't spend half that."

She handed him a twenty dollar bill. "Bring me what you don't spend. And mind your P's and Q's."

"What's that?"

"Mind your manners, behave yourself and watch your language."

"Oh, I will, Mom." He flashed his mother a bashful smile. "She's really pretty."

"No doubt, you're a handsome young man." She proudly fussed with his jacket, brushing off some lint and adjusting the fit. "Don't forget the flowers. They're in the ice box."

"Oh yeah, the roses," he said. "Thanks for reminding me, Mom. Oh, and thanks for the extra ten."

"You have a good time tonight."

"I'm going to sure try."

On the way to Kathy's house, Sean smiled, remembering the day he played gumshoe, sneaking in and out of doorways, ducking behind cars, following her to an upscale neighborhood after a football game. He felt a little disappointed that she lived in an enormous modern two story house with bay windows. It was perched on a knoll, with sweeping views of the airport and the San Francisco Bay.

Rounding the corner to her house, he stopped for a final grooming and studied his reflection in the side mirror of a parked car. Lips cocked and brows furled, Sean rumpled his hair for the mussy look and ambled up the tree-lined street. A shiny, new red Cadillac was parked in the driveway next to a well-manicured lawn. Standing at the massive entryway, staring at the doorbell, he suddenly began feeling nervous. He looked at his wristwatch and rang the doorbell. He could hear the chiming through the oak doors as he peered through the beveled glass and saw a towering giant coming towards the door. He tensed when the door swung open and he looked up at the huge grizzly bear of a man. His neck was thick and his head, almost the size of a basketball, reached the top of the doorjamb. The man was so big, Sean felt like a dwarf.

"I'm Kathy's father. You must be Sean?"

Intimidated by her father's massive size, Sean took a deep breath, and whimpered, "Yes, I am. Nice meeting you, Mister Svenson."

Kathy's father scrunched his jaw and looked suspiciously at Sean, leaving him feeling like a puny weakling.

In a hoarse, gravelly voice, her father blared up the winding spiral staircase, "Kathy, your date is here."

"Tell him I'll be right down," Kathy hollered back.

Her father extended his large right hand and said, "Come inside, Sean. No need for formalities. Name's Carl."

"Nice to meet you, Mister. I mean Carl," said Sean, doing his best to conceal the pain he felt when Carl squeezed his hand with an iron grip.

"She might be a while."

"I don't mind," said Sean, following the stalking hulk across the foyer into a spacious study, noticing that her father walked with a limp.

"Have a seat. Can I get you a Coke or Pepsi?"

"No thank you. I just had a big dinner."

Engaged in small talk with Carl, Sean sat glancing at the sports photos and framed newspaper clippings hanging on the wall. A worn-out and faded football jersey with the number 16 was draped over a chair. Sports trophies and front-page headlines lined the bookshelves. *Wow, a quarterback, a genuine gridiron hero.* Sean was even more impressed by the black and white photo of Carl mounted on the wall. He was wearing a decorated Air Force flight jacket and standing beside a World War II bullet-riddled fighter plane. Another picture of Carl, wearing a judge's black robe, holding a gavel, really intimidated Sean.

Sitting down on a swivel chair behind an oak desk that was cluttered papers and folders, Carl asked, "You're Irish?"

"Yes, and Scottish and a lot of other stuff."

"Isn't Sean the same as John?"

"I think so."

"Kathy's habitually late. Though I do expect she will be down sometime tonight. Have you given any thought to what you would like to do after you're finished with high school?"

"I'm going to college to study archeology. I used to think it'd be fun being a skywriter. But now I think going on digs and discovering ancient relics and artifacts would be even more fun. Maybe I'll be an astronaut."

"Want to fly to the moon, huh?"

"Yeah, that'd be a blast."

"Play any football?"

"I'd like to but I'm not big enough. Most of the players on the team are twice my size."

"You look to be nearly six feet.

"Almost, I'm 5 foot eleven and a half."

"That's the perfect height to play tailback or halfback. Your size gives you the ability to cut and dodge, zigzag until you find the hole and sight your path, then spurt downfield in the open and streak into the end zone. There's no better feeling than when you cross the goal line and score a touchdown, especially the game-winning touchdown."

"I can imagine. Heck, all those trophies and pictures, you must have been a darn good quarterback."

"I love the game," Carl said. "Then I racked my knee. I know Buddy Spencer the varsity coach at your school. We played college ball together at Michigan State. Buddy's a good man. If you'd like, drop by some weekend and we'll toss the pigskin around."

"That'd be neat. I'd like that."

"Ta-da," said Kathy, gliding into the room with a beaming smile. "I'm ready." She was wearing a sleeveless blouse and a frilly skirt over layers of crinolines, and her golden hair was bouncing over her frail shoulders.

Sean stood up and held out the bouquet of pink roses. "Wow! You look terrific."

"Thank you," she said, taking the flowers and holding them to her nose. "They're very pretty and smell nice. Sorry for taking so long."

Sean's legs were rubbery and on the brink of buckling as he stared foolishly at her and stammered, "That's okay."

Kathy's father gave Sean a stern look. "You have her home by eleven sharp."

Sean nodded. "You bet, mister, I mean, Carl."

"See ya, Dad," said Kathy before she kissed her father on the forehead. "Would you mind putting these flowers in a vase?" She handed them to her father and turned to Sean. "What's the weather like outside?"

Walking into the foyer, Sean said, "Foggy. Maybe you should wear a coat."

"It's not far, I'll wear a sweater." She pulled a cardigan from off the hat tree and handed it to Sean. A strange sensation swept over him when she slid her arms into the sleeves and he adjusted the collar, while trying his best not to stare at her cleavage.

Listening to the jingle jangle coming from the silver bells, tied to her shoelaces, all Sean thought about as they walked along the sidewalk down the hill was getting the courage to take her hand. Kathy, bursting with wholesome vitality, talked nonstop about football that Sean could hardly get in a word.

"I'm sorry," she said. "I've been blabbing up a storm."

"That's okay. You're so gussied up, I feel like a bum. I should've worn slacks instead of jeans."

"You look dapper and your sport coat matches your shirt."

"It would've been better if I'd worn a tie."

"Don't be silly," she said. "Oh, thank you for the roses. Pink is my favorite color. You're very sweet."

He smiled. "You really look pretty tonight."

She fluttered her lashes and blushed, appearing flattered. "Thank you. Are you still in the Sea Scouts?"

Surprised, he stuttered, "How did you know I'm in the Sea Scouts?"

"I saw you dressed in your sailor's uniform once. And I know that you snow ski and you're good."

"Huh, how do you know that?"

"Girls like to gossip. A couple of my girlfriends have seen you skiing at Squaw Valley. They told me you're a daredevil."

"Really, well, I do love speed and getting airborne."

"Aren't you afraid of getting hurt?"

"Naw, I've been skiing since I was a little kid."

"I've never been skiing."

"You'd love it."

"I surf. My dad got me a surfboard last Christmas."

"Cool, I surf a little."

"It's hard," she said, "I'm always wiping out. But I'm catching on and surfing's so much fun. I don't ride the big waves or hang ten. Not yet anyway. Right now, I prefer smaller waves until I get the hang of balancing."

"That's the key to any sport. Surfing is all about balance. Maybe we could go sometime?"

"Sure, I'd like that."

The way she looked at him, holding her hand became an even greater challenge, but his fear of her abruptly pulling her hand away prevented him. Arriving at the movie theater, Kathy mingled with her girlfriends while Sean stood in line waiting to purchase their tickets, and trying to come up with something witty to say when they were seated up in the balcony.

When they walked through the doors into the lobby, grasping her hand was now an obsession for Sean. A loud rumble of inane jabber came from the mostly teenage audience when they entered the dimly lit theater and made their way up to the loges. Row after row, Kathy stopped to chatter with her girlfriends, leaving Sean feeling like a gawky goofball. Halfway up the aisle, she leaned over to say something to a girl when Scott Simpson had the audacity to grab her hand and pull her toward him. The brash jerk stared at Sean, tweaked his lip in a cocky grin as he whispered in Kathy's ear. Sean was feeling an overwhelming impulse to yank the clown out of his seat and throw a knee into his crotch, when the lights faded and Kathy grabbed Sean's hand. The warm touch of her fingers sent him into ecstasy and calmed him down. Holding his hand, Kathy hurried up the aisle to the back of the balcony and to Sean's disappointment, she let go of his hand, plunging him into misery as they walked sideways along the row of seats.

Seated below the film projector, a stream of grayish-blue light flowed over their heads. When the newsreel filled the screen, Sean focused his attention on regaining possession of her hand. He remembered how soft and warm it felt. He pretended to watch the screen, but his eyes were focused on her legs as she straightened her skirt and rested her hands on her lap. *This is not the time to be bashful. You coward, you chicken. This is absurd, it's ridiculous. It's hilarious. Half the kids here are snuggled together and you don't have the guts to hold her hand. Take the initiative, this ain't amateur night, you bumbling fool.*

When *Rebel Without a Cause* ended and the lights came on for intermission, Kathy turned and smiled at Sean. Dreamy-eyed, she clasped his hand and they talked about the movie as surges of high voltage electricity shot through Sean's body. He was on the brink of short-circuiting when she squeezed his hand and set it on her lap. His central nervous system went wacky when she rested her seraphic head on his shoulder. Whiffing the scent of jasmine coming from her lustrous, silky mane, Sean slipped into heavenly bliss.

A sudden surge of bravado swept over him and he let go of her hand and draped his arm over her shoulder.

She turned and smiled at him. "I really liked James Dean," she said. "He was cool and so young. That was such an awful tragedy."

"I know, it's a darn shame," said Sean, still trying to come up with something clever to say, but drawing a blank. "I like Sal Mineo and Natalie Wood is dynamite. Hey, would you like something to eat, a soda pop or some candy or ice cream?"

"A Coke," she said. "Oh, and some taffy; no, skip it. I'd better not. I'm on a diet. Popcorn is better."

"A diet; gee, you're perfect the way you are."

"Thank you. But I have to be careful. I'm trying out for the varsity cheerleader squad when I'm a junior next year."

"Really, that's nifty. Do you want salt and butter?"

"No salt, but a splash of butter sounds peachy keen." She smiled and reached for her purse. "Let me give you some money."

"Heck no, I'm buying."

"You've heard of Dutch treat, haven't you?"

"No, what's that?"

She looked surprised. "It means we each pay for ourselves. In this case, you bought the tickets, so I pitch-in and pay for the snacks."

"Well, this is one date where I buy."

She looked a trifle peeved. "I was only offering to help."

His heart sank. "I'm sorry. I just want to treat you."

"That's sweet, Sean."

His equilibrium restored, he gently squeezed her hand. "I'll be back in a jiffy."

Standing at the jam-packed snack bar, Sean was mapping out a strategy to kiss Kathy when he felt a slap on his back.

"You get to first base yet?" Sal asked.

"I'm working on it right now. Are you here with Marylou?"

Sal shrugged. "Naw, I came stag."

"What happened?"

"She brushed me off with another lame excuse. And I couldn't rustle up a date at the last minute."

"Again, that's too bad. Have you seen Arnie?"

"He's up in the loges making out with Caroline. That babe is hot."

"That'll be one dollar and forty cents," said the freckle faced young girl behind the counter.

Sean paid the girl and grabbed the carton of goodies. "I've got to get going, see ya tomorrow, Sal."

"What's with the popcorn? I told you that chicks dig chocolate bonbons," said Sal. "Get her something sweet."

"She's on a diet. Can you believe that?"

Coming up behind Sean, Arnie jabbed him in the back and said, "Sorry for spooking you, Sean. But that chump, Scott Simpson just walked up and sat next to Kathy. Thought I'd come down and tell you."

Almost dropping the carton," Sean blurted, "That fries my butt. I'm going to pulverize that turkey's face."

"Now you're talking," said Sal.

"You're darn right," said Sean, "this is the last straw. That brash scumbag is going down for the count. The jerk had the gall to grab Kathy right in front of me."

"Stomp that slime bag's butt," said Arnie.

Enraged, Sean charged up the balcony aisle and felt relieved when he saw Kathy jabbering with girlfriends and not Scott Simpson. Her friends waved at Sean and left when he sat down beside her. He wanted to ask her what the heck she was doing talking to Scott Simpson but let it drop.

Sean held the bag of popcorn as they chewed and sipped soda pop. Intermission ended and they were watching *Gidget* when their greasy hands were reunited. When Kathy rested her head on his shoulder, the wafting aroma of jasmine swirled in his love crazed mind.

"You look just like Sandra Dee," he said when the movie ended and they were waiting for the crowd to thin before leaving. "You two could be twins."

Kathy sat upright and glowed. "Really, you think so?"

"No kidding. You're even built like her."

"She's my favorite actress. She's real and down to earth, none of that pretentious phoniness. And she's so beautiful."

"So are you."

"You don't have to say that. It's not true."

"But it's the truth."

"Now you're lying."

"No, I'm not. It's true. You really remind me of Sandra Dee."

"You don't have to say that."

A surge of electric current rushed up his spine. "You're even more attractive than her."

"I think you're very good looking," she said, giving him a jaunty smile.

Sean's mind went blank.

"Nobody's ever told me that I'm attractive," she said. "It's always cute, pretty or the girl next door."

"There's nothing wrong with being beautiful."

"Do you prefer blonds or brunettes?"

"It wouldn't matter. I suppose I'm partial to blonds. But it's not important. You could have brown or black or red hair. What's important is a person's spirit. You have plenty of spirit and a great smile."

She looked deep into his eyes. "I like you and I've really enjoyed reading your poems, especially the one about you dreaming about me on a beach. Is that true?"

"It sure is. You've been in my dreams a lot lately."

A pressure relief valve opened and vented the pent-up steam that had been burning inside Sean as they got up and made their way down the steps.

Outside the theater in the misty coastal breeze, they mingled with friends for a short while. Feeling relaxed and a bit brave, Sean slipped his arm around her slender waist when they began a slow promenade under a crescent moon to her house. Laughing, their legs moving in unison, she put her arm around his waist.

Sean loved feeling the movement of her swaying hips nudge against his palm as they walked up the stairs to her house. Standing at her front door, Kathy swirled her tongue around her glossy pink lips and stared invitingly at him. He wrapped his arms around her and pulled her tightly against him. She was on her tiptoes, her lips puckered and her eyes lambent, when the drapes abruptly slid open. Through the window, Carl glared at Sean. Sean froze.

"Dad, for heaven's sake," Kathy lashed out. "Would you please get away from the window?"

The curtain jerked shut.

"Don't mind my dad," said Kathy. "He always waits up for me. He's a worrywart. Thanks for the swell time tonight."

"Did you really have a good time?"

"Yes, honest."

"So did I."

"Really?"

"Heck, I've wanted to ask you out since junior high school, but I didn't have the nerve until now. Sometimes I'm a real lump-head."

"No you're not. You're a nice person. I can't stand guys who paw me and think they can do whatever they want. Do you ever go to the Magnolia Teen Center dances?"

"Sure, a lot but I've never seen you there."

"I'm always too busy. Would you like to go sometime?"

"Heck, yeah, I'd like that a lot."

"Well, I'd better get inside. My dad has a thing about curfew. He comes unglued and has a conniption fit if I'm a minute late."

Kathy stood up on her toes and fluttered her lashes and Sean pressed his lips to hers. Bells tolled in his head and every cell in his body tingled as they kissed. He felt lightheaded and his knees were wobbly when their kiss ended and he took a deep breath.

Kathy's teeth gleamed like pearls in sparkling water as she grasped the doorknob. "Well," she said, thank you for the swell time. It was fun."

"Pleasant dreams," he said in a squeaky voice. "See ya."

After Kathy said good night and closed the door, Sean leapt down the stairs and cart-wheeled across the lawn. Traipsing along the sidewalk, he felt as if he was levitating ten feet in the air. Voltaic energy surged throughout his body and he sang, "She kissed me, oh, yeah, she kissed me."

5

AFTER SEVERAL DATES and becoming juniors, Sean and Kathy began dedicating their Friday nights to teasing each other on the bustling dance floor at the Magnolia Teen Center. They were working-up a sweaty lather, bopping to Buddy Holly and the Crickets singing *That'll Be the Day* on a hot Friday night when Kathy looked at Sean admiringly and said, "You've really become a very good dancer. Have you been taking lessons?"

His ego inflated, Sean spun her around and replied, "My sister and some of her girlfriends have been teaching me."

"They've done a great job, I'm impressed."

Sean felt grateful that his sister and her friends had taken the time to teach him the be-bop, and kept bugging him until he learned to take the lead.

He twirled Kathy around and said, "Thanks. How about you? I mean, you're an incredibly good dancer."

"That's because I studied ballet and gymnastics, mostly the floor routines. I love the parallel bars."

He slid Kathy between his legs, pulled her back up and said, "I've seen you, but you're even more fantastic on the pommel horse and you're a heck of a good ice skater too. I used to watch you at the ice skating rink. That's why you have such terrific legs."

"You really think so?" Kathy said as Sean whirled her around. "I've always thought they were too skinny."

His eyes were riveted on her chest when she began to shimmy and he said, "They're perfect. You look exceptionally sexy tonight." He felt relieved that she appeared to take his comment in stride.

Kathy's tendency to take the lead irked Sean, but after a few tug of wars, he won out. The tempo slowed and Sean steered her toward the dark shadows of the dance floor, away from the scrutinizing eyes of the volunteer den mothers. In the darkness, dancing cheek to cheek, they slowly did the pelvic bump and grind to *This Magic Moment* by the Drifters. His body tingled when she began nibbling on his earlobe and gently suckling his neck. When their favorite song *In the Still of the Night* by The Five Satins began playing, Kathy turned flaming hot and gave him a monkey-bite. With daring aggressiveness, she slid her tongue between his lips. As they were circling their tongues, Sean decided to step across the boundary and boldly placed his hands on the backside of her tight-fitting pedal pushers. She quickly brushed his hands away, stepped backward and shoved him hard on the chest.

"Are you crazy," she angrily said, raising her hand as if to slap him.

He quickly grabbed her wrist and said, "I'm sorry, Kathy, I got carried away."

She yanked her hand away and looked around. "Not here," she said. "Not in front of everybody."

Sean vowed to savor those few seconds his hands touched her soft rear for the first time. The words 'not in front of everybody,' kept repeating in his swirling mind as he gently took her arms and pulled her back to him and said, "Don't be mad."

"I'm not mad. It's human nature, but not in front of the entire student body. Anyway, I'm partly to blame for French kissing you and getting you so worked up."

Sean's eyes shifted to her pear-shaped breasts. *You need to get a car and take this sweet lady to lover's lane.* A sharp poke on Sean's shoulder interrupted his concentration and he turned and saw Scott Simpson.

"Mind if I cut in?" Scott asked with a smug grin.

Sean released Kathy, raised his arms and clenched his fists. "Over your dead body," he shouted.

Scott punched Sean hard on his upper shoulder, knocking him to the floor.

Kathy stepped up and slapped Scott across the face. "You get out of here this instant," she yelled, "you two-timing creep."

Sean gathered his wits and swung his leg into Scott's ankles, dropping him onto his back and quickly sprang on top of him. Scott grasped Sean's throat in a stranglehold. Sean's face was turning a mild shade of purple when he smashed his fist into Scott's face. But Scott wouldn't let go of Sean's neck and Sean punched him in the face two more times just as Sal and Arnie burst through the encircling crowd. Arnie pressed the heel of his shoe on Scott's nose and hollered in a threatening voice, "Let him go, Scott. Let him go or I'm gonna crunch your nose."

Kathy removed a pump from her foot and swatted Scott on the back of his head. "Let him go, you miserable swine," she screamed, kicking him in the ribs. "You're going to kill him."

Scott released his hands from Sean's neck and Arnie removed his foot as Scott's two cronies rushed over with their fists cocked.

As Sean and Scott stood up, an angry den mother charged over and huffed, "What's going on here?"

"Break this up now," shouted another den mother, "or I will call the police."

"This ain't the end by a long shot," said Scott in a low voice before he and his two cronies sauntered away.

"There's no need to call the cops," Sean told the den mothers. "It's just been a misunderstanding."

When things settled down, the den mothers left and Kathy went to the bathroom with Caroline and Marylou to freshen up. Sean turned to Arnie and Sal and told them, "That low-life dimwit had the gall to try and cut in while Kathy and I were dancing. That punk's face is gonna look like mince meat after I've stomped his butt."

"Action is better than words," said Arnie.

"Let's grab something to drink," said Sean, "I'm thirsty."

Seated at a table drinking Coca Colas, Sean finished explaining to his friends what had happened.

"That guy's a loser," said Sal.

"Yeah, Sean," said Arnie, "you need to put an end to this."

"You walloped that butt-face good," said Sal.

"I ain't finished," said Sean. "I'm calling him out on Monday after school. Spread the word. I want the whole school to see that scumbag go down. That's enough talking about that butthole. Kathy told me she invited Caroline and Marylou to a slumber party tomorrow night at her house. You guys up for a panty raid?"

"What about her dad?" Arnie said. "He's a judge."

"He's going to the ballet with some hot-shot attorney babe. Anyway, I'm asking Kathy to go steady later tonight. I've got the ring."

Arnie and Sal grinned wildly and slapped Sean's hands. A few minutes later, Kathy, Caroline and Marylou joined them at the table. Sal's girlfriend, Marylou, soft-spoken and shy, and had an olive complexion, high-cheekbones, big dark eyes, and silky long black tresses that fell to her waist. Arnie's gal, Caroline, was a lusty, blue-eyed blond bombshell. She always wore tight-fitting skirts, low-cut blouses and flaunted her huge boobs. Kathy's cheerful, extroverted personality had Marylou and Caroline giddy and giggling.

When the dance ended, Sean wrapped his arm around Kathy's waist as they walked outside and mingled with friends. After saying goodbyes, Sean walked Kathy home. Arriving at her front porch, Kathy said, "I'll just be a minute. There's something I want you to take a peek at."

When Kathy went inside, Sean sat on the wooden bench. He was staring at the full moon when she came back out with a binder and cuddled next to him.

"It's a book report I wrote for my English class," she said. "It's due on Monday. I thought because you enjoy reading so much, you could read it and tell me what you think. It's only three pages."

"Sure," he said, taking the binder. "Oh, wow, *The Raven*. That guy Poe's a scary dude."

"You think so too? I couldn't sleep after reading it."

Sean laughed as he perused Kathy's report. "I know what you mean. I just finished reading *The Pit and the Pendulum*. It was real creepy."

"I read that one too," said Kathy. "Ugh, it was disgusting. All that man wrote about is death, rats, dungeons, torture chambers and other morbid stuff."

"I think Poe was more of a poet than a storyteller. You can tell by his name, Poe, poet. Kind of like that guy Longfellow, his poems are long."

She smiled. "Yeah, you're right. Longfellow's probably tall and lanky."

"A lot of writer's change their names. I think Poe was on drugs when he wrote that stuff."

"There's no doubt in my mind he was high on something," she said as Sean flipped the last page. "I don't know what, but Poe was definitely spaced out. Well, what do you think?"

"It's good, very good, and the grammar and punctuation and everything are excellent. This is A+ material."

"You really think so?"

"I know so."

They played a couple games of tic-tac-toe and hangman while talking about her dog, Snotty and staring at the waxing bulbous moon.

"You know, Kathy," said Sean, "your dad's some kind of swell guy. I really like him a lot. He's taught me so much these past couple weeks. And what a throwing arm he has. Heck, your dad can hurl that pigskin half the length of a football field."

Kathy stopped doodling and scooted away a little, staring excitedly at Sean. "There were hordes of scouts coming from big cities with professional football teams to watch my father play in college, and hounding him to sign a contract.

"I'll bet."

"You should see all the invitations they sent him, inviting him to go to training camp. The money they offered him wasn't chicken feed either. It really hurt my father when he injured his knee. He was lucky the Air Force took him. It helped him to forget."

"That's too bad about his knee. But if he had a bum knee, how'd he get into the Air Force and be a fighter pilot?"

"My father wasn't a pilot, he was a flight navigator."

"But that picture of him inside the cockpit."

"Oh, that. A friend of my father's took it."

"Really," said Sean. "Anyway, I've really enjoyed tossing the ball with your dad. At first I felt a little intimidated but that was mostly because he's so big. He must wear a size 14 or 15 shoe."

"You were close, he wears a size 16."

Sean paused in thought. "I don't want to probe, but I saw a picture of a blond woman in your dad's office. She sort of resembles you. Is that your mom?"

Kathy grimaced. "Yes."

"She's really very beautiful. How come you never talk about her?"

Kathy moved away and placed her fingers on her cheek. "What is this, family interrogation night?"

Sean shrugged. "Gee whiz, no. Look. I'm really sorry if I was out of line."

Kathy turned somber. "No, you weren't," she said. "It was my fault. I'm sorry for harping at you like that. It's just hard for me to talk about my mother." Tears began rolling down her cheeks and she blurted, "My mother was killed in a head-on collision when I was just a toddler."

Sean's brow furled and his mouth opened wide. "Oh my God, I'm sorry, how tragic. That's so sad."

With trembling hands, Kathy fumbled for the Kleenex tissues she always kept in her bra. "It was far worse than sad. It was horrifying. I was in the car, but she had me harnessed in the backseat and I didn't get hurt. Not even a bruise or a scratch."

Taken aback, Sean held her tightly. "I'm so sorry about your mom, but I'm sure glad you weren't injured."

She wiped her eyes. "So am I. I was lucky to have survived. My father's never gotten over it. I still find him crying in his study sometimes while he's looking at my mother's pictures. He rarely talks about her. He says the pain is too much for him to bear. I don't even remember her. I try to avoid talking about her because it hurts me too much. I get all gooey-eyed and shaky. Like now."

"I'm sure glad you look like your mom. She's a knockout. You sure don't look anything at all like your dad."

A faint smile appeared on Kathy's face as she wiped her teary eyes. "My mother had an exceptionally beautiful body too. My father has an old scrapbook inside his desk. You should see her in a swimsuit. I'll show them to you sometime."

"I'd like that."

"What about your family? "You never talk about them."

"They're cool."

"What does your Father do?"

"He's a music teacher at a private boy's school. My mom's an artist."

"Your father's a music teacher and your mother is an artist. That's so cool."

"My mom's pretty good too. Actually, she's a lot better than good. She's having an exhibit at a gallery in the city in a couple of weeks."

"Really, I would love to go."

"Sure, but I'm not telling you my parents are anything like Ozzie and Harriet."

"Sounds like you have an interesting family," she said, snuggling against him. "It must be wonderful having two brothers and a sister. Sometimes I feel like an orphan. What's your sister like?"

"She's pretty cool. She's head over heels in love, dating some jock law student at Cal Berkeley. He asked her to marry him a few weeks ago. The guy completely wigged out when my sister told him she wants to wait until she's got her doctorate and is teaching."

"I'd like to meet your family."

"Oh, you will. You should be proud of your dad. He's a superior court judge."

"I am. He's just a little too strict. What about your younger brothers?"

"Oh, those two, they're a couple of rascals, always getting into mischief." He rested his hand on her thigh and looked at her eyes. "Why did you call Scott Simpson a two-timer?"

Kathy's face distorted. "We dated. But it was a long time ago."

So that's why he has it out for me. "You went out with that sleazebag?"

"It was back when I was a freshman. He used to be a nice guy until he started hanging out with those two creepy friends of his. My father couldn't stand him. Anyway, I found out he jilted me."

Surprised, Sean said, "He jilted you."

"Yeah, one of my girlfriends saw him out with a biker chick on a night we had a date and he called and canceled. He told me he had the flu."

"You ever think of becoming one?"

"Become a what?"

"Ah, a biker chick."

Kathy slid away and stared at Sean with a curious expression. "Why would you dare ask me such a question?"

"Because I saw you at a gang-fight once," he said.

Kathy's face flushed. "Oh, God, that was so horrible. I only went that one time because I really dig motorcycles. I've never gone to another one. That's the only time I ever went, I swear."

"I believe you. You don't come anywhere close to fitting the image of a biker chick."

She looked at him strangely. "What were you doing there?"

"Oh, ah, some old friends were nagging me to join up with their gang. But after seeing that brutal warfare, it didn't seem like fun."

"You're too much of a goody two-shoe to be in a gang."

Sean took in a deep breath and said, "Hey, I've been meaning to ask you something."

"What's that? Kathy said, tickling his rib cage."

Laughing, he said, "I was thinking maybe you and I could-ah-sort of, ah, go steady. What do you think?"

Her eyes beaming like shooting stars, Kathy threw her arms around him. "I was beginning to wonder if you'd ever ask me."

Smiling brightly, Sean said, "I guess that means yes?"

Kathy stared at him. "Only if you promise that you'll never cheat on me."

"I would never do that."

"If I ever find out . . ."

Sean cut her off. "Hey, I would never hurt you. I'm not a cruel guy."

"Then okay."

Grinning wildly, Sean dug his hand into his pocket and brought out a ring. "It's nothing fancy. Do you want to try it on and see if it fits?"

"I'm not going put it on my finger," she said, unsnapping the gold chain around her neck. "I'll wear it on my necklace." She took the ring and slipped it alongside her favorite amulet. It's beautiful, where'd you get it?"

"My sister gave it to me for Christmas. It's my birthstone."

Looking surprised, Kathy said, "It's a black opal. You're a Scorpio?"

"Yeah, but I'm not much into that astrology stuff. Are you?"

"A little, I read my horoscope. Does the O stand for O'Malley?"

"That or October," said Sean. "Your birthday's July 13th. What's your birthstone?"

"Ruby or pearl, I'm a cancer," she said, putting on the necklace and snapping the hook and eye shut. "I love it. You're such a sweetheart." She kissed him.

"Kathy," said her father from the doorway, it's after 11.

"Yes, Dad. I'll be in a minute."

Sean squeezed her hand and said, "I'll see you tomorrow."

*　　*　　*

After school the coming Monday at Orange Park, Sean and Scott began circling each other with their fists raised in front of nearly the entire student body. Ten minutes later, Scott Simpson, bloody and badly bruised, with black eyes and a bloody nose, finally dropped to his knees and surrendered. Unscathed, except for minor gashes on his knuckles, out of breath and drenched in sweat, Sean thrust his arms triumphantly over his head as Scott's two cronies lifted their friend onto his feet. Sal and Arnie wrapped their arms around Sean in congratulations.

"Not bad for your first fight, Sean," said Sal.

"I hope it's my last."

"You nailed him good with that wicked uppercut," said Arnie.

Caroline and Marylou came over and patted Sean's rump. "That jerk won't be messing with you anymore after the pummeling you gave that creep," said Caroline, handing Sean a wet towel.

"Your hands are fast," said Marylou. "Where's Kathy?"

"She told me she wasn't coming," said Sean.

*   *   *

By late spring of their junior year in '61, Kathy and Sean were inseparable lovebirds. Kathy made the varsity cheerleading squad and Sean got serious about football and took up Kathy's dad on his offer to coach him the elementary fundamentals of playing the game. Considering his age, Carl was in terrific shape, except for his gimpy knee. He was rigid about training. Even on the days when the quicksilver hovered in the sweltering nineties, Carl had Sean running backwards and sideways, smashing through dummy blockers until he was debilitated from exhaustion.

*   *   *

One blistering Saturday afternoon, Kathy, wearing short shorts and a pink satiny blouse, pitched in to play center and seductively bent over. Wiggling her hips, she poked her upside down head from between her legs and made a funny face. Sean felt weak at the knees when she snapped him the ball. Getting past Carl, a hulking giant wasn't an easy task. Still recovering from Kathy's saucy snap, Sean rolled left, faked a pass to her and cut right, but Carl Svenson had an abundance of patience and executed a body-slamming, head-jarring tackle. The man was a tackling machine without mercy and ably covered the entire field.

With the help of Carl's rigorous training, Sean developed some fancy footwork and was finally able to dodge the hulk's merciless tackles. It was only when Sean turned to watch Kathy limbering up, performing leg stretches, jumping jacks, deep knee bends and the splits along the sidelines that Sean lost concentration and got knocked senseless by Carl.

At the end of practice one Sunday afternoon, Carl launched into a harangue on the advanced tactics of playing football. They were sitting on the first row of the grandstands, wiping their foreheads with cold towels as Sean listened intently to Carl.

"Not bad, Sean," said Carl, looking pleased. "You've made very good progress these past few weeks."

"Thanks, Carl," replied Sean.

"You still need to work on bringing your legs up higher. Bring 'em up to your neck. Keep bulking your thighs, and pack some more muscle on those calves."

"I'm working hard on it."

"Good," said Carl, "Keep at it. All in all, I'd say you've made remarkable improvement. But you still have a tendency to signal the direction you're going to run. Defensive backs only need to look at your eyes to find out which direction you'll be running. Same as they do when they watch the eyes of the quarterback to know where he's going to throw. The inexperienced ones always tend to follow the receiver they're going to throw to." Carl took a long swallow of ice water. "What it boils down to is this. Use deception. Never look at where you're going to run. Follow your blockers and keep looking for the hole. When you find it, look in the opposite direction. Tuck that pigskin tight to your ribs with two arms and bring those knees high up to your chin, like the pistons on a locomotive."

"Yeah, that's the way Jim Brown runs. He's the greatest."

"There's another fellow by the name of Ernie Davis," said Carl. "Most people know of him as the 'Elmira Express.'"

"Yeah," said Sean excitedly, "I've heard of him. He goes to the same college that Jim Brown went to, Syracuse, doesn't he?"

"Right," said Carl. "'The Elmira Express' has the same running style as Jim Brown and is just as elusive. I'd put money on that man winning the Heisman Trophy."

"Wouldn't that be something if he teamed up with Jim Brown? Wow, Cleveland would be unstoppable."

"There's a good likelihood that might happen, Jim Brown discovered the Elmira Express. They both use their legs like battering rams, knocking down any lamebrain defensive back foolish enough to get in front of them."

"I've seen Jim Brown run," said Sean. He runs over blockers like they're padded dummies. He's the best."

"And remember, if they come at you sideways, straight-arm them in the kisser. You want to be the hero, don't you?"

Sean nodded. "You betcha, Carl."

"Hey, you two," hollered Kathy, wearing shorts and a frilly low-cut blouse, jogging in place on the sidelines, "why don't you guy's wrap it up. It's scorching out here in this desert."

"Hold onto your britches, Kathy," said Carl. "We're almost done, take another lap."

Sean began laughing when Kathy went into her duck walk routine.

Carl looked Sean straight in the eyes. "I talked with Coach Spencer. He told me if he feels you've got what it takes and can cut the mustard, he'd be willing to try you out on the varsity squad. Don't forget to run right at those defensive backs like you're fearless. And always keep an eye out for the hole. Be elusive. Look at what you're doing right now, staring at my daughter," said Carl, snarling at Sean. "It's a dead giveaway that you're thinking something naughty."

"Huh, I am not," said Sean. "I'm just watching her do her patented penguin walk. She's funny. She's . . ."

With a stern expression, Carl interrupted him. "Don't give me that hogwash. I was your age once. You don't think I know what's on your mind."

Caught by surprise, Sean squeaked, "It's not though, I mean, I like your daughter a lot."

Carl patted Sean on the shoulder. "You're a good kid, Sean. Don't mind me. I'm her father."

Feeling slightly relieved, Sean said, "You don't need to talk to Coach Spencer on my behalf. I appreciate your offering but I'd like to make the cut on my own."

"Suit yourself."

Sean continued working out with Kathy's father every weekend until football tryouts began. He stuck to his diet and held to his bodybuilding regiment. Working out with Carl for a couple months, Sean easily made the cut on the varsity first-string squad. But Coach Spencer had his pet favorites and put him in at right guard in the season opener against Westmore High School.

The afternoon of the game, Sean jogged onto the field, looking over at Kathy on the running track, getting the crowd pumped up by vigorously jumping the splits and tossing her pompoms high in the air. When she looked over at Sean, he blew her a kiss before two male cheerleaders grabbed Kathy and catapulted her in the air. Jacked-up with excitement, yet feeling disgruntled for being put in the game as a right guard instead of a running back, Sean joined the huddle. After the quarterback called the play, pumped up in a fever, Sean took his position at the scrimmage line. Taking a deep breath, he dug his cleats into the turf, planted his knuckles on the grass and looked up at two of the most ferocious faces he had ever seen.

"I had your sister last night," one of the opposing linemen snorted. "She was a mighty fine lay."

Ignoring the linesman's disgusting remark, Sean held his position, said nothing and listened for the count.

"I had her too," the other sneering lineman growled. "Spun your sis round, buttered her plump rump and took her from the backside. Then your sister took the whole shaft and gobbled it down. Whacha gonna do about it, boy?"

Something inside Sean's head snapped and he totally lost control. In a rage, he lashed out at one of the spiteful linemen, landing a right uppercut to his Adam's apple. The lineman quickly grabbed his throat and slumped to his knees as if in prayer. The other lineman threw a wicked pump kick into Sean's midsection. Sean ignored the pain and pounced on the lineman, grabbing the brute's jugular. Within seconds, Sean's teammates dragged him off the screaming player.

Ejected from the game, Sean bowed his head, striding to the sidelines where he got a verbal ass-chewing from Coach Spencer.

"You fell for that old ploy!" The outraged coach shouted after Sean finished explaining what the two linemen had said. Coach Spencer's face matched the color of his red hair when he said, "You're suspended for a mandatory two games. You need to learn to control yourself. Now get out of my sight and take a shower."

Sullen-faced, with his head tilted down, Sean slinked off the field. Overcome with humiliation, he didn't bother to look over at Kathy.

A few days later, Kathy's father walked into the dining room where Sean and Kathy were sitting at the table doing their homework.

"It happens to the best," said Carl, resting his broad hand on Sean's shoulder. "Don't let it get you down."

Sean looked up at him, feeling embarrassed and dejected. "I appreciate everything you've done for me, Carl. I wish I could tell you what those ton of lard's said to me, but it's unmentionable. I lost it."

"I can well imagine what those bullies said. Whatever they said, I'm sure I've heard worse. It's a common tactic used to draw a player off sides. Coach Spencer is still fuming, but he'll get over it. Hang in there, you'll get another shot."

"What's a Pythagorean theorem?" Kathy asked.

"The hypotenuse," said Carl.

"Yeah, C is equal to the square root of A squared plus B squared," said Sean with a proud grin.

Kathy threw her hands up. "You two are geniuses."

*   *   *

Three games later, at halftime, South City's rival, Jefferson was ahead 13 to 7. Sean sat on a bench along the sidelines, grumbling and hoping for redemption. Late in the fourth quarter, consternation set in, and Sean began thinking of walking off the field and quitting the team. Coach Spencer had never looked once at Sean during the game.

With only a few minutes remaining in the game and Jefferson still ahead 13 to 7, the starting halfback for South City twisted his ankle and hobbled off the field with the aid of two teammates, grimacing and groaning in pain. Sean, sitting with his head lowered on his splayed fingers, abruptly sat upright. Hope began to rise in his heart. Sean knew he had a chance when he looked over at Coach Spencer, standing with his hands resting on his hips, scowling over at him. Just as Jefferson was about to punt from its own thirty-five-yard line, Coach Spencer called a time-out and curled his index finger at Sean for him to come over.

Midway through the pep talk, the coach said, "If the ball hangs too long, signal for a fair catch."

Sean nodded and continued to pay close attention to what the coach was telling him.

"The kid punting has a tendency to nail line drives," said Coach Spencer. "If he does, take it up the right hash marks, follow the iron curtain, then slant left and follow those bulldozers, Bradford and Toomey."

Sean nodded.

Coach Spencer frowned. "We have two time-outs remaining, and the two-minute warning. Don't fumble the frigging ball. You do, and you won't have a chance to make water boy next year. Now hustle out there and prove that Carl Svenson knows what he's talking about." Coach Spencer slapped Sean hard on the butt.

Running onto the field, Sean stopped and turned. "You won't regret this, coach," he hollered. "You have my word on that."

His prayers answered and jacked-up, Sean sprinted to the twenty five yard line and stood the lone punt-returner. His adrenaline was pumping at maximum velocity when the punter kicked a spiraling boomer that hung in the air for what seemed over a minute. Calling for a fair catch never entered Sean's mind. The ground below his feet rumbled and shook like an earthquake was taking place. The sounds of bodies crunching and helmets smashing up field echoed in his ears, yet Sean remained calm, trying desperately not to blink his eyes, concentrating on the trajectory of the ball. The spinning football floated down from the black sky, past the blinding flood lights like a hallowed gift from the heavens, dropping straight into Sean's arms. The pigskin tucked tightly against his ribcage, he remembered the coach's instructions and took off up the sideline, his eyes frantically searching for Bradford and Toomey's numbers. Racing in a zigzag pattern, he slanted left and straight-armed the first would be tackler hard on his shoulder. He broke another tackle and found Bradford and Toomey, and his eyes searched for the miracle hole. He looked right, and cut left and hurtled straight at the punter. Running with his knees coming to his neck, Sean rammed a straight-arm into the punter's chest. Toomey, charging like a bull, sideswiped an oncoming tackler. Bradford leveled another rushing tackler to the ground. Sean faced only one more foe coming sideways at him. Shifting into overdrive, Sean threw his palm into his chest, knocking him to the ground and proceeded to sprint into the end zone. Out of breath, he raised the football victoriously over his head, spiked it hard onto the turf and went into an Indian war dance.

The extra point aced perfectly through the center of the goal posts. The final score: South City 14, Jefferson 13 and the roar from the students in the grandstands erupted. His head buzzing, Sean got his first taste of being carried off the field. A few moments later, yelling, "You did it, I don't believe it," Kathy raced wildly up to Sean and vaulted into his arms. Locking her thighs around his waist, she attacked his neck with hickeys before passionately lip-locking him.

"After you've changed, hero boy," said Kathy, jumping out of Sean's arms "let's go to Papa Joe's. I'll spring for pizza; my dad gave me twenty bucks." She ran to her fellow cheerleaders.

"Hell of a great run, pal," said his wide receiver team-mate, Arnie, slapping Sean hard on the back.

Swinging a camera, Sal ran up to Sean and said, "I'm putting your kisser on the front page of the school paper. "You're making the headlines with the shot I got of you dancing in the end zone."

After ten minutes of backslapping and shaking hands, Sean sprinted to the locker room with his teammates.

6

WALKING WITH HIS pals Arnie and Sal after school let out, Sean was scanning the front of the school for a silver Chevrolet Impala. Sean clinched his fists and raised his thumbs when he spotted his sister Heather sitting in the front seat of his mother's car, waving at him.

His heart thumping wildly, Sean coolly told his two friends, "Time's come, fellows, I've gotta split and get my drivers license."

"Good Luck," said Arnie. "And don't forget to keep both hands on the steering wheel at all times."

"And keep your eyes on the road," said Sal. "Don't get distracted by some hot looking babe wiggling her fanny as she's crossing the street, wearing a see-through blouse."

"Yeah, yeah," said Sean, snapping his fingers. "See you cats later. If I get that car, I'll cruise by your pads tomorrow morning and pick you guys up."

Cracking his knuckles, Sean scurried across the street to his sister.

"Hey, birthday boy," said Heather, glossing her fingernails, "big day, huh?"

"Been a long time coming, sis," said Sean, getting inside the car. "Sixteen's a day of jubilation. I really appreciate you coming today." He reached over and turned on the radio.

"Please, Sean. No music. It disturbs me while I'm driving."

He turned the radio off. "You're worse than mom."

Heather blew on her nails, put the jar of fingernail polish in her purse and started the motor. "I can't concentrate with the radio on. Music distracts me and muddles my mind," she said. "How does it feel to be turning sweet sixteen and maybe getting your license on the same day?"

"Ain't no maybes, sis."

"You must be excited."

"Hard to describe," he said. "Exaltation comes to mind. My head's been flying high in the clouds since I woke up this morning. Mind if I drive, I've got my permit with me?"

With a distraught expression, Heather said, "Only if you promise not to drive fast. It makes me nervous."

Sean smirked. "Don't worry, sis, I'll maintain the speed limit. I promise."

Half an hour later, Sean drove into the parking lot of the Department of Motor Vehicles in San Mateo.

"Good luck, little brother."

"Don't need it, sis," he said, parking the car, "I have the book memorized."

Having read the DMV manual over a 100 times, Sean only missed one question and passed the written test. Heather was sitting on a bench reading a paperback copy of Robert Grave's *The White Goddess* when Sean walked outside with the driver examiner. The way the man was leering at Sean when he got inside his mother's car, caused his stomach to cramp. His fingers were so sticky that he fumbled inserting the key into the ignition and started the engine. The man didn't speak a friendly word, except to give Sean directions when he drove out of the parking lot onto the two lane road.

"Make a right turn at the stop sign," the man said in an authoritarian voice, carefully scrutinizing Sean as he scribbled notes on a clipboard.

"Yes, sir," said Sean, putting on the blinker and making a right turn signal with his left arm. Stopping at the crosswalk, he made sure to look in both directions before proceeding.

Ten minutes later, keeping a close eye on the speedometer and a complete basket-case, Sean drove back to the DMV for the parallel parking test.

As many times as he had practiced parallel parking without coming anywhere near to touching a cone, Sean cringed each time he came close to one.

"Swell job parking," the man said when Sean put the gear lever in park and shut off the motor.

Taking a deep breath and wiping the sweat from his forehead, Sean said, "Thank you."

"As for your driving, you were driving a little too slow. It's much safer to move along with the flow of traffic."

The tension mounting and on the verge of breaking out in a rash, Sean stuttered, "Well, ah, I mean, did I pass?"

The man scribbled some notes on the sheet of paper and said, "Yes, you did."

Sean's body convulsed and he raised his fist as the man signed his name and handed him the sheet of paper. After the examiner exited the car, Sean waved the paper and grinned wildly at his sister before he got out and walked inside to take the vision test.

Looking at the eye chart after waiting in line for almost an hour, Sean covered his left eye and blinking and squinting, he read every letter and passed the eye exam. Wound up like a ticking time bomb, he felt the impulse to stick out his tongue at the female clerk behind the counter. He restrained himself and forced a smile. The clerk politely returned his smile, took his hand and pressed his thumbprint on his temporary driver's license.

Grinning wildly at the girl as she handed him the license, he said, "Thank you."

He thrust the license over his head and began proudly waving it at the people around him, before he turned and walked away. The urge to scream his lungs out was overwhelming as he pushed open the glass door and sprinted over to his sister, sitting on a bench.

"Did you pass the eye examination?" Heather asked.

"With flying colors sis," he said, basking in glory and flashing the temporary license in front of her nose as they walked to the car. "I wasn't sure about that examiner, the way he kept glaring at me and not saying a word rattled my nerves to no end. I thought he was doing it intentionally so he could get his jollies by flunking me. I was wrong. Hey, thanks for coming today, sis."

"I've actually enjoyed it. I've gotten to know you so much better. You're not such a dumbbell after all."

"Would you cut out the name calling?"

"You used to be. But watching you park the car changed my mind. You never even came close to touching a plastic cone. I couldn't have done any better. I was a nervous wreck when I took the parking test."

"So was I, sis, I'm driving and springing for burgers."

"You don't have to," she said as she sat in the passenger seat. "I came here because you're my brother and I love you. Just be careful and watch the speedometer, you have a tendency to drive too fast. You'll have a pile of tickets stacked up in no time if you don't slow down."

Pumped up, Sean sat behind the wheel and fired the engine. "Bug off. Hey, one more itsy bitsy favor?"

"What?"

"There's this snazzy car that's for sale. I've been looking at it for a couple weeks on the way home from school. It was there a couple days ago and then yesterday it was gone. It's probably been sold."

"Don't be so pessimistic. Maybe the seller was showing it to someone."

Sean shifted the gear lever into drive and drove out of the parking lot. "That's what I've been hoping all day."

"Let's drive by and find out."

"You sure you have the time?"

"I'm finished with school and I don't have to work today," she said. "Just don't drive fast."

"Yeah, yeah."

A short while later, Sean made the sign of the cross just before he rounded the corner and saw the car that had been catching the attention of his wistful eyes every time he walked by it.

"Yahoo, it's still here," Sean shouted, parking behind an old Ford and putting on the emergency brake.

"You mean that beat up old jalopy?"

"Not that junk heap," said Sean. "The consummate dream machine parked in the driveway. She needs a good scrubbing and a can of polish."

Heather's eyelids raised and she said, "You mean that blue Chevy convertible?"

"Yessiree," he said as they got out of the car, "a baby blue '57 ragtop. Ain't she a beauty?"

"It's dreamy all right," she said. "But how can you afford it, the sign says a thousand dollars?"

"Negotiation," said Sean. "Last night, I tallied the money I've been socking away from my paper route, my allowance, caddying, and mom and dad's presents for getting good grades. I had more than seven hundred buckaroos saved up. And last night, dad kicked in a hundred dollars. I got 800 smackers in my pocket."

"Gee, Sean, that's terrific. That is if you can get the owner to lower the price."

"You haven't seeing nothing yet, sis," he said. "Wait till I come out jangling the keys after some wheeling and dealing. Say a prayer that someone's home."

"I will. If you need some extra money, I can help a little. I have a few extra dollars saved."

Sean's eyes lit up. "Really?"

"Sure, as long as you promise to pay me back as soon as you can."

"After you took the time help me out today, of course I'll repay you when I get paid next week. I would never rip off my big sister."

Sean paused, staring at the ultimate dream machine in a moment of silent fascination.

After they thoroughly scanned the interior through the windows and seeing that there wasn't a tear in the upholstery, Heather said, "The inside looks brand new."

"Only a minor ding on the bumper and not a scratch on the paint," said Sean. "Be back in a flash."

"Good luck."

"Thanks," he said and bolted up the terrazzo steps. He drew in a deep breath and excitedly pressed the doorbell. A burly middle-aged man, with a bulging beer belly, a thick handlebar moustache, coveralls and wearing a Giants baseball cap opened the door. The man invited Sean inside and the two chatted briefly before Sean got down to some serious bartering.

"I know the sign says a thousand dollars, but I have 800 greenbacks of cold, hard cash in my pocket," said Sean, triple emphasizing the word cash.

Chuckling, the man snapped his suspenders, scratched the Vandyke stubble on his chin, and thought a moment. "Hmmm, it's a start," he said. "Don't you want to take it for a test drive?"

"Sure. Does the radio work?"

"Brand spanking new, am, fm, too. Just had two new speakers installed in the deck behind the back seat. It's a great sound system."

"Cool," said Sean, looking down at the car through the open window. "How's it run?"

"Like a champ. Just had her tuned up. New tires, clutch, brakes, battery, and I just filled up the gas tank this morning."

"Everything work?"

"Yep, even the clock. Hate to let it go, but my old lady ain't too fond of stick shifts. I'd consider knocking off fifty bucks. Make it 950 with no guarantees. You buy it as is."

"I just want to look at the engine and listen to it. See how many miles it's got. I'll know after I drive it."

"She's just breaking in, sonny boy."

Thinking he could scrounge a hundred from his sister, Sean crossed his fingers and countered, "How about nine hundred bucks, right now, cash?"

Sean's anxiety began to mount as he watched the man fiddle with his suspenders in thought.

Snickering and nodding, the man said, "No sense haggling over a measly fifty bucks. You said cash, didn't you?"

"You bet," said Sean, feeling the urge to jump, but maintaining and casually taking out a wad of bills from his pants pocket. He removed the rubber band and spread the bills on the table.

"They almost look brand new," the man said. "You didn't print these yourself, did you, young man?"

Sean choked. "You mean counterfeit, heck no. I got these fresh from my bank yesterday."

The man studied Sean carefully and counted the bills. "Just checking, you can't be too careful nowadays. Seems you're short a hundred."

"Oh, I need to go get the rest from my sister." Sean swooped up the money and stuffed it in his pocket. "I'll be right back."

"Mind leaving a deposit, some folks are coming by in bit to peek at it. Sort of an act of good faith."

"Sure, is a hundred okay?"

"That's fine. You got a driver's license?"

"Yeah, and insurance," said Sean, showing the man his license and insurance papers.

The man glanced at the temporary license and said, "Why you got this today and it's your birthday."

"Yeah," said Sean, handing him a hundred dollar bill. "Be back in a jiffy."

Outside the front door, Sean shot down the steps and bustled across the street to where his sister stood leaning against their mother's car. He dropped down on his knees in front of her, made the sign of the cross, and said, "Can I borrow a hundred dollars?"

"A 100 dollars," Heather balked with a shocked expression. "That's a lot of money, Sean."

"I know, but I'll repay you. You have my word. I'll get mom to loan me fifty as soon as we get home and give it to you. I promise. I'll you the other fifty next week."

"You'd better."

Standing up, Sean embraced Heather and said, "You're an angel."

When they got back from Heather's bank, Sean ran up the stairs and carefully studied the bill of sale, service records and the pink slip. Everything appearing in order, he darted downstairs. The burly man followed behind and stood grinning as Sean paused to catch his breath.

The man lit a cigar and handed Sean the keys. "Go 'head and fire her up."

The very moment Sean cranked the ignition and slowly revved the engine, listening to the purr, he knew it was his lucky day. Sean pulled the hood release handle and the man raised the hood.

In a flash, Sean was bent forward staring at the nearly 300 horsepower V8 engine, "Wow," he said, "the motor's spotless."

"Just like I said, kiddo, you're getting' the deal of a lifetime. Your sister's a knockout."

"Yeah, I know."

"Take her for a spin. Just bring her back in one piece."

Sean waved for his sister to come over and lowered the hood. He went around and unlocked the passenger door and held it open with a big smile. "Ladies first."

"A manual transmission," said Heather, sliding onto the front seat.

Sean closed the door. "Four on the floor's the only way to fly, sis. Listen to her purr."

"Can you drive a stick-shift?"

"It's as easy as counting to four."

After the man showed Sean how to lower the top, the moment he had strived for since becoming a teenager arrived when he slid behind the wheel. He placed his palm on the gear shift knob and slipped it into reverse, feeling as if he was transcending into a higher state of consciousness. His eyes roamed slowly along the dashboard, visually caressing every dial and button.

Sean looked at the burly man and said, "Be back in a few minutes."

The man grinned and moseyed back to his house as Sean slowly let up on the clutch and rolled onto the road.

Sean turned on the radio and grinning wildly at Heather, he dialed in Chuck Berry singing *Johnny B Good.* "We're gonna be flying, sis. I'm legal and free as a bird." He shifted into first and roared away.

"Slow down, Sean," Heather angrily shouted when Sean popped the clutch at a stop sign. "That's illegal." She reached over and turned off the radio. You're scaring me, Sean."

Stepping on the gas and racing through the intersection, Sean joked, "Stop means Spin Tires on Pavement."

"Please, Sean, stop driving so fast."

Sean shifted into fourth, let off on the gas and said, "Okay, relax."

Ten minutes later, feeling exultant, Sean rolled up behind their mother's car. "Well, what do you think, sis?"

"I like it, but you drive way too fast."

"Yeah, sure."

"I'm serious, Sean. There are serious consequences for speeding. Before you know it, you'll have tickets piled all over your desk and your license will be suspended."

"Hey, back off, will ya?" Hearing the irritation in his voice, Sean said, "I'm sorry. I'm really grateful for your taking the time to help me today and loaning me the hundred smackers. After I take care of the paperwork and pay the man, you and I are having lunch, my treat. See ya in a bit."

The balance paid and the bill of sale signed, Sean looked at the man, and said, "Thanks, Mister Simpson."

Sean's excitement continued rising as he watched the man sign the pink slip. He almost flipped out when the man handed him the keys and said, "She's all yours, kiddo, have fun."

His body covered in gooseflesh, his adrenaline surging faster than the current of a raging river, Sean ran down the stairs.

Jingling the keys, he said, "Follow me to Papa Joe's."

"Don't forget," said Heather, "you have to register it in your name."

"I know that."

His head high, Sean held the door open for Heather at Papa Joe's Pizza joint and followed her to a table. After pigging out on burgers and French fries, they walked out the front door an hour later.

"You be careful," said "and lighten up on the gas pedal. You don't want to wreck your new car. Accidents are costly."

"Stop worrying, sis. Thanks again for everything, you're a sweetheart."

"Do you have any money for gas?"

"Tank's full and I've got pocket change."

"Where are you going now?"

"Cruise by Arnie's and Sal's. I want to watch them eat their hearts out when they see this baby."

Hell-bent on showing off his hot ragtop, Sean zoomed over to Arnie's house. Arnie was in the driveway working on the engine of his black '56 Plymouth Fury when Sean pulled into the driveway.

"Well, what do you think?" Sean said, rolling alongside of Arnie's car.

"Pop the hood and let me see what she's got."

Sean got out and raised the hood. "She's got 283 cubic inches of pure thrust and four on the floor," he said. "Check it out."

Staring at the chrome air filter over the carburetor, Arnie didn't seem overly impressed. Arnie pulled back the linkage and revved the engine. "She's not too shabby," he said, "but this engine's starving for fuel. Get rid of that chintzy two-barrel and get yourself some thirsty dual AFB quads, then get a high-rise manifold, Mallary ignition, a Duntov turbocharger and you might have yourself a screamer."

"I'm saving up right now," said Sean.

"And pick up a high performance Duntov camshaft. You'll need big lobes if you want to keep up with *FireEater* said Arnie, referring his car.

Yellow, orange and red flames shot across the fenders, hood and doors of Arnie's black *FireEater*. Arnie had removed the original hood ornament and replaced it with a fire-spewing dragon.

Grinning, Sean said, "I'm going to. And when I'm done souping her up, you'll be gagging on *Lil Reb*'s exhaust fumes. Just you wait."

Arnie laughed. "That'll be the day."

A half hour later, Sean finished sketching the name *Lil Reb* on the front fenders of his car. Arnie took two cans of beer from his dad's wet-bar and they shook the cans. When the pressure built up, they christened *Lil Reb* with sprays of frothy foam and guzzled the cans empty.

"I'll see ya, pal. I'm cruising over to Sal's pad then I got to get home for supper. After that, I'm heading to Kathy's pad. I can't wait to see her face when she sees *Lil Reb*."

After showing off his car to Sal and a quick dinner at home, his mother loaned him fifty bucks and Sean paid his sister.

With the top down and the cold wind slapping his face, he shifted into fourth, imagining how his idol felt, the great Formula One race car driver, Juan Manual Fanzio, when he crossed the finish line as Sean raced to Kathy's house. He parked in front of her house, revved the motor and honked the horn. With a wild-eyed smirk, he watched Kathy peek out of the bay window before she ecstatically blew through the front door, flew down the steps, and skipped merrily to his car.

Kathy's eyes were wide with excitement when she blurted, "Holy smoke, birthday boy, a ragtop. How totally cool; and I love the color, baby blue. It makes the birthday present I got you look like peanuts." She leaned down and gave him a quick kiss. "But gosh, how on earth could you afford it?"

Beaming proudly, Sean got out of the car and said, "Been saving up for it since I became a teenager and my parents chipped in." He opened the door for her. "Come on, angel face, slide in and let's take a thrill spin."

"I'd better tell my dad and grab a warmer coat, it's a little chilly." She took a gift-wrapped package out of her light jacket pocket and tossed it on his lap. "I hope you like it. I'll be right back."

Sean was standing beside the car, proudly holding the door open when Kathy came skipping over to his car a couple minutes later.

"So gentlemanly," said Kathy, zipping up her light blue parka and sliding to the middle of the front seat. "You haven't opened your present."

"Thought I'd wait for you," he said, running around the car and sinking into the driver's seat. She squeezed tight against him, as he ripped off the ribbon and tore off the wrapping paper. He opened the box and pulled out a leather sunglass case.

"Ray Ban's."

"There's more."

He set the case on the dashboard and stuck his hand deeper into the box. "Oh wow, kid leather gloves and a silk scarf. I don't know what to say except, thank you." He placed his fingers on her cheek and kissed her.

"Put them on."

Sean wound the scarf around his neck, slipped on the gloves, put the shades on and looked in the rearview mirror.

Shaking his head and grinning foolishly, he turned and stared at Kathy, "You're something else, sweetheart. I feel like . . ."

"A dashing pilot," she said with a bright smile.

He grinned and said, "Fanzio at the start line."

After they kissed, Sean fired the engine and slowly drove away. At the first traffic signal, he popped the clutch and peeled rubber. He waited for a lull in traffic before he downshifted into second gear, punched the gas and raced off. He slammed the gearshift into third and caught rubber. Shifting into fourth, he said, "Hold on tight, its blast-off."

Sean cranked up the volume when Chuck Berry began singing *Roll over Beethoven* and slammed his foot on the pedal

"Sean, please, you're scaring me, slow down."

"Oh, sorry," he said and backed off on the pedal.

A short while later, he pulled off Skyline Boulevard into lovers' lane, overlooking the festoon of bright lights that stretched from San Francisco to San Jose. He parked beside the withering ancient oak tree he had carved their initials the night he stole his mother's car. They sat enchanted listening to Roy Orbison belt out *Crying* from the rear speakers.

His arm around Kathy's shoulders, Sean said, "The prettiest girl in school and now a '57 dream machine. I must be leading a charmed life."

"You're sweet," she said. "That's why I'm so stuck on you. I absolutely adore your new wheels. It's dreamy and fast. It's the ultimate."

He smiled broadly. "You haven't seen nothing yet, sweet cakes. This baby's going to fly after I've souped her up. What do think of the name *Lil Reb*?"

"It's nifty, but I was thinking *Baby Blue* when I first saw it."

"Really, so did I, that or Eliminator, or Invincible. I can change it to *Baby Blue* if you want."

"No, I'm starting to like *Lil Reb*. It has a nice ring."

He grinned. "Hey, you can drive her later tonight if you want to."

She looked tempted and then shook her head. "I'd better not. I only have a permit. Besides, I haven't learned how to drive a stick-shift. I've only driven my father's car. And it's an automatic."

Sean shrugged and said, "It's a piece of cake. I'll teach you. It's real easy. I had a brainstorm on the way here. "It's a fantasy I've had since the day I first fell for you. What do you think about us riding through the tunnel of love at *Playland at the Beach*?' I'll have you home by ten, I promise." He stared at her with eagerness.

She giggled and snuggled against him. "Fantasies, tunnel of love, you're cuckoo," she said. "Okay. But nine, no later. It's a school night, and you know how my father gets when I'm a minute late. I also have a lot of homework tonight."

They were cruising alongside of the Pacific Ocean on the Great Highway when Kathy asked him, "Have you thought about what college you're going to after we've graduated?"

"I haven't thought about it. What about you?"

"My dad thinks he can get me a scholarship at his alma mater, Michigan State. He says it has a good law department."

Sean's heart felt a strange twinge. "Law," he said. "What side of the law?"

"What do you mean?"

"Would you defend or prosecute?"

"Defend, I suppose. You know, justice for one, justice for all. After some experience, I want to be a judge like my father."

"I like that."

"What will study in college?"

"I honestly don't have a clue," he said. "Maybe art, but unless you become famous, nobody buys your work. Most artists die starving or committing suicide. I can't imagine myself taking orders from a boss. Maybe I'll be a pilot and spend my life flying around the world."

"That sounds so neat," she said with a bright smile. "Maybe I'll skip law and become a stewardess and we can fly together."

He grinned. "I wonder what it feels like to make-out at twenty-thousand feet inside a cockpit."

"Sounds dreamy," she said as Duane Eddy was singing *Rebel Rouser* on the radio. "Hey, they're playing your car's theme song."

He stared at her with adoration. "Geez, you have such a sweet face. I'm positively the luckiest guy in the world to have you as my girl."

She stroked his cheek, kissed him and whispered softly in his ear, "That's why I love you."

Hearing Kathy murmur the words "I love you" always made Sean feel warm and tingly inside. It seemed like the sound of sweet music being sung by angels from high above in the cosmos. But getting the words "I love you" to flow out of his mouth was a mammoth undertaking for Sean.

With each effort, he instantaneously developed lockjaw. Even when they were engaged in heavy petting on the dance floor, the words "I love you" felt anchored by a hundred-pound ball, chained to his vocal chords.

He parked at Playland at the Beach, and they started out the night by smashing into each other, riding the bumper cars and having a blast. A little later, they were licking cotton candy and staring up at the grotesque fat lady cackling in the window. The fat lady's laugh was so horrendous they laughed until they were almost blue in the face. They were still laughing when they stepped into a photo booth and Sean dropped a quarter into the coin slot. When the red light began flashing, they made silly faces and crammed the cotton candy into each other's mouths.

After licking their faces clean, Sean purchased four tickets to the tunnel of love. Inside, he turned and winked at her, thinking his fantasy was about to become reality. Sean's head was in a dream world when they sat in a small car and began rolling along, listening to the wheels clink and clank on the tracks. When their eyes adjusted to the darkness, they tenderly embraced, their tongues swirling around in each other's mouths.

The experience was so enrapturing, they took another ride and the words "I love you" finally floated out of Sean's mouth like a punctured balloon.

She jerked away and stared at him. "Did you mean that or did you just say that to appease me?"

"It just came out. I've never said those words to anyone, except my family. You're the only girl I've ever said that to. It's true, I mean it. I love you."

Kathy quivered and her eyes radiated like blue quasars. "Nobody, except my father, has ever told me they loved me. Do you really mean it?"

He squeezed her arm. "Of course I meant it, I wanted to tell you a long time ago that I love you, but the words wouldn't come out. Now it's easy. I love you."

"It feels wonderful to hear you say that," she said and snuggled closer to him.

There was hardly any traffic on the ride home along the Great Highway. Sean pulled over and parked and they sat listening to the sound of waves crashing as he tried talking Kathy into getting behind the wheel. She was reluctant, but after a considerable amount of coaxing, Sean managed to persuade her to drive a stick shift. After he gave her a couple of demonstrations, she finally scooted over and nervously took the wheel.

"Relax, Kathy. It's really simple. It's all synchronicity and feel. Don't pop the clutch. Let it out slowly. When you feel the car moving, step on the gas lightly and release the clutch at the same time."

"Are you sure you want me to do this?" Kathy said with a hesitant expression. "What if I get in an accident? Why couldn't you have bought an automatic instead of a stick-shift?"

"Automatics are for old fogies and sissies. Don't worry, babycakes, you're an angel and angels don't wreck cars. Now drive."

"I don't have a license or insurance. I only have a permit."

"Don't worry, my parent's put me on their insurance policy and I have a license. You're perfectly legal."

Kathy appeared relieved and slowly let up on the clutch, simultaneously pressing down on the gas pedal. The car lurched and bucked for quite sometime until she caught on to the technique and gained some self-confidence.

At sixty miles per hour in fourth gear, Kathy was bubbling with effervescence. Rolling south along a desolate stretch of road, her confidence increased. The faster she raced, the more invigorated she became. At seventy, she was grinning like a madwoman with her blond hair frazzled and flying every which way. Sean shook his head in delighted wonderment.

The needle was wavering at eighty miles an hour and Kathy kept *Lil Reb* steady between the lines. Her face was so electrified, Sean couldn't keep from laughing.

Seeing three deer standing frozen in the middle of the highway, staring at the car's headlights, Sean jerked up, braced himself and yelled, "Watch out Kathy."

Screaming hysterically, Kathy slammed on the brakes and the car spun around. The rear end collided into one of the deer's with a giant crunch. The deer's hoofs conked Sean on the back of his head when it thumped down into the back seat. The collision helped to slow the car as it jumped the curb and screeched to a halt sideways in a cloud of burnt rubber just short of a sea wall.

"I'm so sorry, Sean," Kathy shouted. "Those deer came out of nowhere. Are you okay? What's wrong? Why are you holding your head?"

"The darn deer's foot clobbered on my head, but I'm alright, just a little dazed.

"I'm really sorry about your head and wrecking your new car."

"It's just the tail end. I can fix it. Look, it wasn't your fault. Those damn deer stopped right smack in front of us."

"I'm not driving anymore."

"Help me get the deer out of the car," said Sean. *"We have to get the heck out of here before the cops come."*

"Is it dead?"

"I think so. It's just a fawn. It won't be heavy."

"Oh, my God," said Kathy, "I killed a baby deer and smashed your new car. I feel so terrible."

"Come on. We've got to hurry."

They got out and walked to the rear of the car. Staring at the mangled rear-end, Kathy raised her hands to her cheeks and yelled, "I've ruined your car."

"The trunks a little buckled and the fender has a ding," said Sean, wobbling his head, and placing his arm around her shoulders. "But it's no big deal. It's fixable. Now let's get the deer out of the backseat."

The corpse was lying on the sand when Sean drove away.

"I'm sorry about all the blood on the backseat," said Kathy as Sean parked in front of her house and shutting off the engine.

"It'll wash off."

"I'll help you."

Concealing his shocked disbelief, Sean said, "Wow, you did super fine driving."

"I was driving way too fast," she said. "Why didn't you say something? Why didn't you tell me to slow down?"

He kissed her lightly on the cheek. "I guess it was because I was feeling so exhilarated, watching you get jacked up like that. You looked like a rocket-woman whipping through a wind tunnel."

"I feel awful."

"Don't, it wasn't your fault," said Sean.

Brushing the tangles and knots out of her hair, Kathy asked, "So, when do I get to meet your parents?"

He laughed. "Real soon, I promise."

"You always say that. You told me you would take me to your mother's art exhibit and you didn't. What's up?"

Sean lowered the volume and thought a moment. "My parents get along great except when my dad goes out to jazz joints and jams all night. He's been going out a lot lately. I don't want to bore you."

"You're not boring me. It's interesting."

"Why do you say that?"

"Because it's real," she said. "Not make believe or pretend or all that phony bologna you see on television. That stuff is for shallow-minded people. My head is solid, not hollow. Now, go on, I want to know more about your family. You never talk about your parents or your sister or your brothers. Do you think I'm probing?"

"No," said Sean. "My parents get along fine most of the time. It's only when my dad comes home in the middle of the night that my mom freaks out."

"You're fortunate your parent's are creative artists," Kathy said. "Arnie and Sal are always raving about how much fun they have jamming with your father. What instrument does he play?"

"My dad plays most anything, horns, drums, guitar, piano and harmonica. I like it best when he kicks butt on the sax, he can really wail. He's got soul. He calls it white soul."

"I'd like to hear him play."

"You will," said Sean. "He can really belt out the blues. If anyone heard him singing without seeing him, they'd think he was a Negro. He has a deep raspy voice. It doesn't sound contrived either, it flows naturally. And he can pick those steel or gut guitar strings with the best of um. The way his music ebbs so smoothly, makes my head drift into a state of euphoria. I reminisce about all the times I used to sit listening to him play when I was a little kid. They're precious to me. My dad pulsates with energy."

With an irritated expression, Kathy asked, "When can I hear him play?"

"We could go on a Friday night. He moonlights at upscale jazz clubs in San Francisco. But he prefers sleazy joints like the Blackhawk in the Tenderloin. Minors are allowed."

"I want to hear your father play and see your mother's paintings."

"Your dad's looking out the window. Maybe you should go in."

"I've a few more minutes. The way you describe your father, I know he's great. Tell me about your mother's artwork. What does she paint?"

"Mostly mountain landscapes, lakes with lots of trees and flowers, and other similar sceneries."

They sat in the car with the top down while Sean told Kathy about his parents' until her father slid the curtains back and forth for the third

time. Sean walked Kathy to the door and gave her a good night kiss. He
blew her a kiss into the cool night breeze when he got back to his car.

At a little past midnight, Sean lay in bed unable to sleep. He was
pondering the temptation to get inside Kathy's bedroom. His hormonal
juices raging, he dressed, grabbed a flashlight and snuck out the window.
Ten minutes later, he coasted his car across the street from Kathy's house.
Not seeing a single light on inside her house, he got out of the car and
quietly closed the door. After gathering a handful of small pebbles, he
climbed on top of the fence and began tossing the pebbles at her bedroom
window. A few minutes later a dim light lit her room. He snickered when
he saw her shadow at the window and watched her slide the frilly drapes
aside. Shining the flashlight on Kathy when she opened the window, he
saw that she was wearing pink baby dolls.

With her finger held vertically over her lips, Kathy softly said, "Are
you completely daffy? What are you doing down here? It's almost one in
the morning."

"I couldn't sleep," he said in a low voice, "all I could think about is
you."

Her voice urgent, she said in a soft voice, "Have you gone bonkers,
Mister Tweaky? My father will beat the living daylights out of you if he
finds you here at this hour."

"Live dangerously, be brave," he said. "Look, I only want to come in
for a minute."

Kathy appeared shocked and said, "Come inside my bedroom? You
really are crazy. I don't believe this. You can't come in my room. I'm
serious. I dread what my father would do to you. Probably beat you to a
pulp. Now scram out of here before I'm grounded forever."

"Your dad would never come into your bedroom in the middle of the
night," he said, forcing himself not to grin.

"He's probably listening to us this very minute. Please go home. I'm
frightened."

"You're paranoid. He can't possibly hear us. We're hardly making a
sound."

"My father's an extremely light sleeper. Now get the heck out of here.
I'll see you at school tomorrow."

Sean didn't budge. Instead he continued to plead until she slowly
appeared to soften.

"Kathy—my sweet winged angel baby—just two minutes. Life's a risk, be daring, be bold. I won't make a peep, I promise. Cross my heart."

Kathy fell silent for a moment and, shaking her head, she finally gave in.

"If my father wakes up and finds you in my room," she said, "we'll probably both be in the morning obituaries."

His ego boosted, he tugged on the downspout and felt it was secure.

"You're not coming up that rickety thing, are you?" Kathy said. "You're liable to fall and break your neck."

Sean ignored her and gripped the downspout tightly, gingerly scaling up to the windowsill on the second floor. Poking his head inside her room for the first time, he did his best to conceal his lustful excitement. Halfway through the window, he inhaled the fragrant bouquet from the strawberries on her desk. With only the dim light from the bedside lamp, they sat nervously on the edge of her brass bed in silence, listening to the ticking of the clock.

He took her hand and softly whispered, "I've never been in a girl's bedroom except for my sister's."

"I've never had a boy in my room."

Smiling and tenderly embraced, Sean's head slowly revolved, looking at all the stuffed teddy bears and Raggedy Ann dolls heaped and scattered everywhere. He glanced at the menagerie of small glass and porcelain animals on top of her dresser and the walls that were papered with pink hearts, ribbons and bows. The scent surrounding her must have been French perfume he figured because she smelled like his sister. Even the silver brush set amongst all the fancy perfume bottles and makeup on the glass-topped vanity reminded him of his sister's bedroom. Embroidered on the down comforter they were sitting on were more pink hearts, elephants and monkeys. His eyes paused at the photograph of the two of them sitting together on the sand at the beach that was wedged in the dresser mirror.

Strange squeaky sounds began to emit from the other side of the door, causing Kathy to squirm. She reached across the bed and switched off the lamp. They were lying on the bed making-out when the glass menagerie and perfume bottles suddenly began to rattle.

"What's going on?" Kathy said in a panicky whisper as the room began to shake and sway.

"I think it's an earthquake," said Sean.

Kathy nervously clung to him and whispered, "Oh, fudge, it is an earthquake. I don't believe this is happening."

"Shh, it'll be okay, it happens all the time. This is quake city."

He put his arm around her waist and held her tightly as the rumble and shaking grew more intense.

"I'm scared," said Kathy, pinching his arm. "Why did you have to come here?"

"I think it's almost over," said Sean as the shaking began to diminish. "It's only a mild tremor."

"I hope so," she said, "I'm a nervous wreck."

When the shaking stopped, they fell back on the soft, feathery quilt and embraced in the midst of silent blackness. They were working up a substantial lather, their breathing becoming heavier, their bodies damp from arousal, when an aftershock struck and knocked the bedside lamp onto the floor. The entire house was shaking and they gripped each other in a sudden surge of panic and shock, and quickly sat up. The loud sound of a door slamming jarred Kathy into a state of terror.

"Gosh darn you, Sean," Kathy whispered, "why'd you do this? I'm scared stiff. You've really botched things up. Quick, hide under the bed. And don't you dare cough or sneeze. My father's most likely coming to my room."

In a matter of seconds, Sean lay quivering underneath the bed on the dusty hardwood floor in fear of his life. His heart thumped like the rapid echoing of sledgehammers smashing against steel. The rumble returned and the room started to shake again. Drenched in sweat, he gulped as much air as his lungs could contain and began to silently pray.

You've gone and loused up this courtship big time. If he finds you here, that big hulk is gonna pulverize the living hell outta ya. You're in for a brutal punishment, you moron. Please, God, don't let this happen.

Several loud knocks pounded against Kathy's door before Sean heard the door slam and the light come on. "Is everything all right, Kathy?" Carl said in a loud raspy voice. "Are you okay?"

"Yes, Daddy," Kathy's voice crackled. "I must have accidentally bumped the lamp when something startled me awake."

"It was an earthquake."

"Oh, is that what it was, said Kathy. "Anyway, it's stopped and I'm fine. Now go back to bed. I have to get up early."

"Why is your window open? It's freezing in here."

"I must have forgotten. Would you mind closing it?"

Feeling squeamish and twitching, Sean covered his mouth, forcing himself not to cough as he watched Carl's bare feet walk across the room and listened to the window bang shut.

A moment of terrorizing silence lapsed when Sean heard her father say, "Sleep tight and pleasant dreams, Pumpkin."

Sean's heart was thumping wildly when he heard the door close and listened to Carl's footsteps fade away. Hearing another door slam shut brought instant relief to Sean. Several long minutes passed before Sean quietly crawled out from under Kathy's bed.

"Get the heck out of my room this instant," Kathy said in a hushed voice as she knelt on her bed. "Go on, hightail it out of here, right now, you nitwit. Get out this instant before I sock you in the face."

"Okay, okay," he said softly, "I'm sorry. I'm going, I'm going. I love you. Can we at least kiss goodnight?"

"Kiss? Are you crazy? After the trauma you just put me through. You get the heck out of here before I slap you."

"What about how I felt?"

Kathy stood up and raised her fists like a prizefighter. "Get your fanny out of here right now," she said, stepping onto the floor and walking over to Sean. "I'm warning you, I'm going smack you." She slugged him hard in the chest. "Scat, scram, now."

"Okay, don't be so riled. Temper, temper."

Sean carefully slipped out of the window and scaled down the drainpipe, grateful not to have been caught. Lying on Kathy's bed with her wearing only a frilly pink baby doll and panties made the night more than worthwhile. A treasure he would cherish for eternity.

7

SENIOR YEAR OF '62 blew in with the force of a gale wind. Dressed as Count Dracula on Halloween night, Sean parked in front of Kathy's house. Watching a group of mothers escort a cluster of costumed children across the front lawn of Kathy's house, he decided see what Kathy's dad was up to. Kathy had mentioned that her father went all out on Halloween. He chuckled when the children charged wildly to the foot of the stairway and suddenly stopped, gaping up at a blood-splattered sign that read, *Welcome to Necropolis*. Blood was dripping along the bottom edge of the cloth sign. Propped to the left of the cobwebbed bay window was a fiendish, fanged vampire. Standing at the right side of the window, was the menacing Creature from the Black Lagoon. Swinging in the air from the porch rafters were wicked demons, spooky ghosts, goblins and skeletons.

Sean remained seated as the kids ran up the pumpkin lined steps to the porch and rang the doorbell. When the door opened, the children yelled "Trick or treat," and excitedly held up their brown paper sacks. Sean jerked in his seat when a loud "Boo," sounded from a speaker mounted on the roof and out jumped Carl dressed as Frankenstein. Amidst the eerie amplified sounds, the frightened children shrieked and stumbled over the piles of bones, stampeding back down the stairs. The kids were clutching their mothers' coats when Carl took off his Frankenstein mask. He smiled and gave the mothers a friendly wave. Dressed in a witch's outfit, Kathy emerged from behind the front door. She was swinging a big bowl of candy, attempting to lure the children back up the steps. After the mothers assured the children it was safe, the kids scrambled back up the stairs and Kathy plunked sweet goodies into each of the children's bags. When the kids scattered towards the house next door, Kathy gleefully pranced down the stairs and skipped over to Sean's car.

"Wow," said Sean when Kathy sat in the car, "you weren't joshing. Your dad did a great job making your house look haunted, and that Frankenstein mask spooked the heck out of those kids. That ghastly thing even gave me a case of the willies."

"My dad loves the boogie man stuff."

"I'll say. You ready to boogie?"

"You bet'cha, she said. "I'm in the mood to shake, rattle and role. My father's girlfriend came dressed as a sorceress. She'll definitely freak-out the next batch of kids."

Kathy and Sean were sprinkled with confetti and Sean's face was smudged with lipstick when they left the Halloween dance early and drove straight to lover's lane. Within minutes after Sean parked under their favorite oak tree, the two were deeply involved in anatomy exploration. Sean's mind was orbiting in a fantasy when Kathy shoved him off of her and said, "Let's not get carried away, Sean."

"You're the one who started it," he said, wretched back to reality after Kathy rebuffed him. "It's incredible how you go from tame to heated passion and then shut off in the blink of an eye."

"Believe me," she said irritably, "it isn't easy. But one of us has to maintain control."

"Kathy, you know I admire your self-restraint, but I don't understand how you're able shut down when we reach the boiling point. It mystifies me."

"Well, you're not the one who's going to get pregnant, are you?"

"Yeah, you're right. It's just that . . ."

"Look, Sean," she added hastily, "it's not that I don't want to, because I do."

Flustered, Sean's eyebrows lifted. "You do?"

"What do think? You think girls don't get turned on."

"You sure do," he said. "It just baffles me how you're able to turn off so fast."

"I have to. If I let you do whatever you want, you'd think I was a slut. Well, I'm not a whore, Sean."

"Kathy, I would never think that about you."

"Virginity is a virtue I cherish, and I intend to preserve mine until I'm married."

Sean cut her off. "Hey, relax will you. I appreciate your prudence. I just don't get how one minute you're on fire and the next minute you're an iceberg. It stumps me."

"Give me a break, Sean," she said in a harsh voice. "I already told you, it's not easy."

"You're right, I'm sorry."

After a short pause, Kathy said, "I hardly see you anymore. You're always working on your car, or snow skiing, or out sailing. Now you're going hunting again and football season has started."

"Wait a minute, sweetie pie," Sean fired back, "what about you? Student Body President, head cheerleader, pajama parties every weekend, sometimes I think your girlfriends our more important than me."

"It's because you're hardly ever around anymore."

"Hey, sourpuss," said Sean, "what do you want me to do, quit the team and stop snow skiing?"

"I didn't say that. And I'm not a sourpuss, I'm just being truthful."

"I'm sorry for calling you that. I'll quit the team if you want me to. But not skiing."

"I forgive you. But you can't quit the team, not with coach Spencer trying to land you a football scholarship. My dad told me some college scouts have been watching you."

"Yeah, he told me?"

"They've been checking you out ever since you broke all those school records in your junior year."

"I know. I can't believe it myself. The other day your dad asked me if I ever thought about playing baseball."

"Baseball!"

"Yeah, your dad wants me to try out for the pitching squad this coming spring."

"Don't you think that's overdoing it? Why not focus on football. So you can excel."

"Why the hassle and all this complaining," said Sean, "I don't tell you how to run your life."

"I'm sorry. You're right. I guess it's good to be versatile."

"That's what your dad always tells me," said Sean. "He's a natural athlete. He throws a baseball the same way he hurls the pigskin, only faster. I can barely see his fastball whiz by the plate. And he's got an arsenal of pitches, a curveball that breaks any which way, a knuckleball that jumps, and a split-finger that floats and dives. And his spitball, man, it's like a fireball. Heck, I never know which way it's going. I just wanna duck and get out of the way."

"My dad's not perfect. He has his shortcomings."

"Why do you say that?"

"He's overly strict. He's almost a disciplinarian and treats me like a baby. I'm almost seventeen and a senior and I still have to be home by midnight."

"He let you stay out till two in the morning on the night of the junior prom."

"That was special," she said, "and I had to plead on my hands and knees. All my friends get to stay out till one or even two all the time without having to beg. It's demeaning. Which reminds me, I had better get home before my dad has a conniption fit."

Sean started the engine and said, "I'm meeting Arnie at the Shell Station where Sal works. We're working all night to get ready for next Friday night's drag race."

"You sure are pumping a lot of time and money into *Lil Reb*. Attaining more speed is all you ever talk about."

"Yeah," said Sean as he shifted into third gear, "maybe so, but you take precedence over everything. Even when I'm working on my car all I think about is you. Getting her up to maximum velocity is secondary, then comes beating Arnie's *FireEater* and Sal's *LoveMachine*."

"You're addicted to speed."

"I'm addicted to you."

"You say that, but you're always breaking promises to me. You promised I'd meet your family. I haven't met a soul. You promised you'd teach me to snow ski."

"Gee whiz, would you stop this bickering. You sure are in a grumpy mood tonight. It ain't even ski season yet. We'll go opening day."

"Promise?"

"Yeah, now give me a kiss and stop all this nagging stuff."

Twenty minutes later Sean pulled up in front of Kathy's house.

"Hey, Kathy, why don't you come with me next Friday night? It's a real gas. Every kid with a fast car'll be there. And you bring me good luck, which is what I need if I'm ever gonna wax Arnie or Sal."

"They don't start till midnight and you know I turn into a pumpkin at the strike of twelve."

He laughed. "Tell your dad you're going to a slumber party at Caroline's or Marylou's house. That's what I tell my parents. I tell them that I'm spending the night at Arnie or Sal's pad."

"What if he calls and I'm not there? Man, I'd be grounded for life."

"Sneak out the window."

Kathy's lashes flickered as if she liked his idea. "I'll think about it and talk to you tomorrow at school."

After Sean walked her to the door and they kissed goodnight, he raced over to the Shell station where Sal worked after school and on weekends. At half past midnight, the station was closed when Sean rolled in and parked in front of an empty hydraulic lift. Arnie and Sal were working on their engines with their faces, hands and work clothes smeared in black grease. Sean slithered into coveralls and walked into the garage. Speed and more speed had become an obsession in their lives. The three kids were forever tearing their engines apart or fine-tuning the timing. Sal's pink '56 Pontiac, the *LoveMachine* and Arnie's *FireEater* were up on the hydraulic lifts. His two pals were working like madmen when Sean walked over to them.

"Old man Patterson's a swell guy for letting us use this place and all this equipment," said Sean.

"The old geezer's a lecher," said Sal. "He's darn near sixty and the back room is plastered with centerfolds. The old fart stays back there most of the day staring at 'um and licking his chops."

"Can you blame him," said Sean. "Think you two can help me get *Lil Reb* up on the racks?"

Sal and Arnie set their tools down and helped push Sean's car onto the rack. Arnie and Sal knew much more about engines than Sean and he depended on their mechanical expertise. Over the past few months, the three kids blueprinted, balanced, bored, stroked, ported, and polished their engines until they glistened. Last weekend, Sean installed a chrome crankshaft, and a high-lobed Duntov racing cam in *Lil Reb*. The weekend before that, he tore off the dual quads and mounted fuel injection atop a high-rise manifold.

"You pick up that Mallory magneto ignition like I told you?" Arnie hollered over the whirr of the three engines.

"It's inside the trunk," said Sean. "I also got a custom Headman header system with four-inch collector boxes. Gonna run straight exhaust."

"How about the Hurst linkage?" Sal asked.

"Yeah, I got that too," said Sean. "I ain't got any money left but I got a gal who loves me."

"Quit the BS and get your butt over here," said Sal. "I need a hand wrenching on this 4-11 posi-traction rear end."

"Hang tight, Sal, be there in a couple minutes," said Sean as he finished unloading the trunk and was raising the lift. "Where's *FireEater's* hood?'" Sean asked Arnie.

"Getting some work done on it." Arnie snickered. "You boys are in for a thunderbolt surprise."

The kids went to work with a maniacal fervor. They muscled in Sal's new rear end, raised the rear shackles and lowered the front-end. They mounted racing slicks on the rear chrome rims of Sal's car. After a short break, they installed the new Mallory ignition, Hurst linkage and Headman headers on Sean's car.

Morning light was beginning to creep over the east bay hills when they gathered their tools and began cleaning up.

"Jeez, Kathy chewed my ass out tonight for not spending enough time with her," said Sean. "How the heck do you guys squeeze in time for precious moments with Carolyn and Marylou?"

"Between basketball, football, *FireEater*, homework, hunting, fishing, and all the other crap I do," replied Arnie, "it's sort of a balancing act, coupled with a lot of juggling."

"Yeah, tell me about it." Sal chimed in. "It's a task, what with running the school paper, soccer and the *LoveMachine*. Ever since I started going steady with Marylou, it seems I don't even have time to take a dump. There ain't no compromising with Marylou. It's her way or no way. I'm still trying to persuade her to come to the drag races on Friday night. She keeps saying it's too risky."

"Ya gotta show 'em who the boss is from the very get go," Arnie said.

"It ain't that easy, Arnie," said Sean. "I've been trying to coax Kathy into coming with me to the drag races for months. She's a basket-case of jitters about her father being a superior court judge. But I've a strong hunch she might come along next Friday."

"That's one thing I like about Caroline's folks," said Arnie, "they don't give a hoot what time she comes tiptoeing home. Well, fellas, it's time to blow this joint."

"Big game next week?" Sal asked Sean and Arnie.

"Naw, we'll slaughter those crème puffs, said Sean.

"It's gonna be a romp," said Arnie, "fifty to zip."

The guys backed their cars out, shut the garage doors and locked the place up.

* * *

Late in the fourth quarter of the opening game against Mills High School the coming Friday night, Sean fumbled the ball on his own five-yard line. Mills recovered and Sean sat on the bench embarrassed and humiliated. He glanced over at Kathy, who was bursting with peppy zest on the running track and vigorously yelling, "Hold that line, push 'em back, push 'em back, way back." For a brief second, Sean felt revitalized watching her. She was so energized, jouncing, kicking her smooth, slender legs high over her head and performing acrobatic loop-de-loops.

With the clock ticking down to less than a minute left in the game, Mills scored a touchdown, making the final score 21-0 in favor of Mills.

After changing out of his uniform and disgusted with his performance, Sean drove alone to Papa Joe's Pizza Parlor. Feeling like a slug and not wanting to talk to anyone, he entered through the back door and sat alone in a booth. He dropped a quarter in the nickelodeon, played his favorite songs and watched Kathy, slurping a root beer float and waltzing from table to table, gossiping with her classmates. Watching her extroverted personality burst with life as she table-hopped brought a slight smile to Sean's face. He cherished the sight until one of Kathy's girlfriends pointed at him and Kathy hurried over to his table and scooted beside him.

"What happened tonight, you fumbled four times?"

"We were playing in a muggy swamp," said Sean. "The darn ball squirted out of my hands. And the foul odor in the air made me sick. Enough said. I don't want to talk about it. I feel dejected enough as it is."

"Case closed. Are you still going drag racing tonight?"

"You bet. Are you coming?"

"I really want to, but I'm a little afraid."

"I understand; you don't have to."

"But I'm going anyway."

"Did you tell your dad that you're going to a sleepover?"

"No, I'm sneaking out the window."

Sean grinned. "Me to. Remember what I told you. When you get home, start yawning the moment you walk inside. And rub your eyes," he said as he demonstrated. "That's what I do. Look sleepy-eyed and say you're beat and going to hit the sack early. It always works for me."

"I'm just worried my dad will come into my room."

"He won't," said Sean, nuzzling her neck. "And don't worry; the rope I got you could lift a dump truck. Make sure you tie it like we practiced. I don't want you falling and getting hurt."

"The bowline knot, right?"

"That or the figure-eight," said Sean.

At a quarter to midnight, Sean snuck out his bedroom window and crept along the patio. Outside in the street, he pushed his car a half block before cranking the motor. Even with heavy steel covers and rubber gaskets bolted to the new collector boxes, the loping throb of *Lil Reb's* heartbeat was just barely legal at normal speeds. He cut the engine a half block from Kathy's home and coasted to a stop three houses away. The evening's light drizzle had diminished and he could see Kathy crouching in the dark shadow at the side of her house as he took the top down. She was barefoot, carrying a raincoat and boots when she boldly dashed out and helped Sean push *Lil Reb*. They were well away from her house when they slammed the doors shut and grinned wildly at each other.

"How come you didn't wait for me to help you?" Sean asked, starting the engine on compression.

"I was antsy," she said, putting on her boots.

"It's so slippery. Did you have any trouble climbing down?"

"No, I wore leather gloves. I was just scared stiff my dad would hear me. I think he's still awake, reading." She moved as close to him as the floor gearshift would allow.

"Well, baby-cakes," he said, "you did good. We're off to the Friday night drag races."

"This is so exciting, it's like were going to a ritual!"

"That's exactly what it is," said Sean, "a Friday night ritual. A flock of dedicated kids with monster engines are gonna be there, all wanting to leave with the reputation of having the fastest car in the county. We're going to raise some Cain tonight."

Arriving at a stretch of highway along Junipero Serra Highway, the thundering racket emanating from the drove of souped up hot rods was near deafening. Sean added to the voluminous clamor when he unbolted the steel plates from the collector boxes and tossed them in the backseat.

"Well," said Sean, getting back inside the car, "what do you think?"

"Holy smoke," Kathy yelled. "Your car is so loud, I can hardly hear you. This place sounds like an airport. What did you do?"

"Bypassed the muffler," he shouted. "This ain't amateur night. These kids take their drag racing seriously."

"How long is the drag strip?"

"A quarter mile; and I mean precisely one-quarter mile."

"Huh," she said, "I can barely hear you with all the racket."

He loudly repeated in a louder voice.

"What about the police?" Kathy shouted. "The police would have fun with me, you know, being the daughter of a superior court judge."

The anxiety in Kathy's loud voice was apparent to Sean and he squeezed her hand. "Relax, Kathy," he said. "Don't get so worked up. There are lookouts all over the place with binoculars and walkie-talkies."

"What if they go kaput?"

"Stop worrying, Kathy," said Sean, "there's nothing to sweat. Everything's covered. The lookouts have whistles and flashlights, just in case. It's fail-safe. Besides, this isn't serious law breaking. We're just a bunch of fun loving kids bending the rules for some Friday night thrills. It's not like we're criminals."

A cute, pixie-faced flag girl wearing short-shorts and holding a pair of green pompoms stood at the start line. The flag girl waved and two hot rods throttled and jerked to the start line.

"Here comes Arnie," shouted Kathy. "Can you believe that glowing tongue sticking out of his car's grill?"

Sean laughed and said, "Straight out of a cartoon." His eyes widened when he saw the blower raised out of a scoop in *FireEater's* hood. "Holy cow, Arnie's running a dang blower."

"What's a blower?"

Sean explained that it was similar to a supercharger, forcing more fuel into the cylinders."

"Where's Sal, I don't see his car?"

"I don't know," said Sean, "but he's here somewhere. A team of Clydesdales couldn't keep that stray cat away."

"How do they know who wins?"

"There are more girls at the finish line with black and white checkered pompoms and stopwatches. The timing is all done with flashlights. This is precision stuff."

Arnie, wearing a surly expression, roared up alongside of Sean's car and revved his engine. It sounded different than Sean remembered and had a distinct high-pitched whir to it.

"You ready to get your butt creamed?" Arnie hollered from his window. He and his lusty girlfriend Caroline were grinning like Cheshire cats.

"Hey, pal, *Lil Reb* is roaring like a lion," Sean retorted. "You two dodo birds are gonna be choking on the smoke these new slicks are going to lay down."

"*Lil Reb* may roar like a tiger," Arnie yelled back, "but *FireEater's* spouting like a dragon."

"You two crème puffs better have brought oxygen masks," Caroline shouted, "because you're going to need them." She made an ugly face and stuck out her tongue.

Kathy grabbed the windshield, raised herself up and yelled, "Blower schmower, you lollipops are about to enter smothersville. You're going to need your prissy, dingaling girlfriend to help push that junk heap across the finish line, Arnie."

The four teenagers became more charged up the closer they moved to the start line, taunting each other.

"Yeah, baby-cakes, you tell those buffoons," said Sean, staring dubiously at the blower and listening to the distinct whine of Arnie's engine. He looked over at Arnie, "You're gonna need Jim Dandy to the rescue after the thrashing you're about to take."

Arnie burst into laugher. "Keep on dreaming goofball."

Still standing and holding onto the winshield," Kathy shouted, "Hey, Caroline, *Lil Reb* is going to blow the socks off your pigeon-toed feet."

"You lump-heads are in for a surprise," Caroline fired back.

Sean pointed at the hood. "What's with the phony blower, Arnie? That some kind of scare tactic?"

"It ain't no fake, buffo. Check it out," said Arnie, slowly pressing down on the accelerator. "*FireEater's* spewing like a flame thrower." The motor's whiny pitch grew higher. "She's running on nitro."

Sean looked at Kathy. "You tell um, Kathy."

"Nitro cilantro," yelled Kathy. "*Lil Reb*'s gonna smother you two in smoke."

The flag girl motioned for Arnie and Sean to move up to the start line.

Sean kissed Kathy's glossy pink lips. "Thanks for the vote of confidence. Hang on tight sweetheart we're about to blast-off." Turning to Arnie, he asked, "Where's Sal?"

"He had a blowout with Marylou and left to take her home."

Sean grimaced. "Not again, those two are always going at it."

Gunning their engines, the two cars lurched to the start line.

Sean focused intently on the green pompoms. "Here goes sweet-cakes, hang on to your seat. It's launch off."

Kathy made some peculiar hand gestures at *FireEater*. "There, I hexed Arnie's car, it's jinxed."

Both cars humped wildly in place, the result of combining forward trust with forced breaking. The tachometer mounted on Sean's dashboard was revving close to six G's when the flag girl jumped up and waved the green pompoms over her head. Overcome with daring bravado, Sean popped the clutch and crammed pedal to metal. The noise turned earsplitting as the tires of both cars were spinning on the damp pavement until they caught traction. *Lil Reb* lurched off the line and squiggled sideways before Sean managed to straighten out. The faulty start gave Arnie a half car-length advantage. At sixty, Sean thought he might have a chance of catching him. At ninety, Arnie started inching away.

When the needle was buried at a hundred and twenty, Sean yelled, "Yeah, baby-cakes, we're gonna break the sound barrier. Get ready for the sonic boom."

Arnie had Sean by a car length when they crossed the finish line. As Sean backed off on the gas, he saw the exhilaration on Kathy's face and wobbled his head.

"How fast were we going?" Kathy asked.

"Don't know," said Sean, parking beside Arnie's car and shutting off the engine. "The speedometer was buried. I'd guess 150 or 160."

"Wow!"

"Hey, Sean," Arnie hollered with a wild grin, "it's time to trade that fool injected pile of junk in for a real car. Gotcha by a car length easy. Go Mopar!"

With a chagrin expression, Sean said, "What can I say, pal, you beat me fair and square. But there's always next Friday."

Arnie cupped his ear with his hand and stuck his head out the car window. "Sirens, it's the fuzz."

"You're right," said Sean. "I can see the red lights coming up the hill. It's time to split the scene and avoid the shakedown. See you later, alligators."

"Let's meet up at Nicky's for burgers," Arnie yelled before he rammed the pedal to the floorboard.

Moments later, bedlam broke loose. Headlights flickered, horns blared, and whistles blew, warning of the impending raid. Kathy fell into a state of panic as hot rods spun brodies, peeled rubber, scrambling and scattering in all directions. Sean and Arnie had a head start and were the first to reach the escape route.

"What if they catch us?" Kathy cried out. "What do I tell them?"

"Relax, Kathy, we're not gangsters or criminals," we're just immature kids having some fun on a Friday night."

"More like defiant misfits," Kathy babbled."

"I like that," he laughed. "But calm down. No cop in his right mind would arrest you. You'd steal his breath away. Besides we're almost scot-free, a clean getaway."

"Oh, no," Kathy screamed, "there's a police car coming up the hill right in front of us."

"I see it," said Sean, making a left turn onto a dark side road. He raced up the street, pulled into a driveway, turned off the lights and shut off the engine.

"I can't stand anymore of this torment. I'm going crazy."

"Would you shut up and get your head down."

"Shut up! Why you miserable . . ."

"I'm sorry, Kathy," said Sean, "I didn't mean it, but would you please put your head down. That cop car was almost a half-mile away. He couldn't possibly make out this car. Would you please duck down, that siren is getting close."

They lay beside each other for fifteen minutes after the sound of the siren had faded.

"Don't you ever tell me to shut up again, do you hear me?"

"Kathy, you were screaming. What if you woke up the people inside the house and they called the police?"

"With the racket this thing makes, I'm surprised they didn't wake up."

Sean got out and quickly bolted the steel plates back onto the collector boxes. Kathy was nervously fidgeting with her hair when Sean got back in the car and embraced her, assuring her that they were safe. But she wasn't completely at ease until they wheeled into Nicky's drive-in and parked alongside Arnie's car' A gleeful carhop skated over and took their orders.

By the time the carhop came back and set the tray of burgers, fries, and root beer floats on the car door, the four teens were rollicking in laughter; the earlier verbal antagonizing forgotten. Not a word was mentioned about Sean fumbling the ball four times.

Going on three in the morning, Sean drove to Kathy's house and parked half a block away.

"I'm scared, Sean," Kathy said nervously.

Studying Kathy's house, Sean patted her on her shoulder. "Don't be, all the lights are off. It's safe. We pulled it off."

"I hope so. But I won't feel comfortable until I'm in bed."

They quietly closed the car doors and Sean walked her to the side of her house.

"I don't remember being so afraid in my entire life when I saw that police coming at us," she whispered. "My father would have grounded me for a year if we'd been caught."

Sean tugged the rope. "We weren't, we escaped."

"What about now. If my father hears me, I'm in deep trouble."

"Would you stop worrying, you're an athlete. Now get up to your room."

She kissed him and put her foot in his clasped hands and Sean boosted her to the top of the fence. "Piece of cake," he said. "Maybe I could come in for a few minutes?"

She grabbed the rope. "Don't make me wet my pants."

He laughed softly and said, "Only joking. You be careful."

Sean watched Kathy scale up the wall with hardly a peep and crawl through the window. *She's something else,* he thought.

8

SEAN WAS SEATED next to Kathy on a chair lift at Squaw Valley on a blustery New Years day late morning when he said, "That was a good warm-up run, you're catching on quick."

"You really think so?"

"Heck, yes," said Sean. "It's only your fourth time you've been skiing. You've gone from the bunny slopes to the beginners. You'll have earned your wings by the end of spring."

"I don't like using the pizza pie to stop," she said. "I want to stop fast like you. How do you do that?"

"You should stick to making the wedge, it's safer."

"I asked you a question."

"Okay. Shift your body weight to your right ski and throw your hips sideways. It's all hip movement. I'll show you. It's easy. A couple more practice runs and we'll move up to the intermediate slopes."

"I want to ski an expert run."

"One step at a time, Kathy, it's early."

Kathy looked at his skis. "Why are your skis so much longer than mine?"

"Speed," said Sean. "The longer the skis, the faster you go."

"I want longer skis. I want to get airborne like you."

"Hey," said Sean emphatically, "I like your enthusiasm, but take it easy. Practice makes perfect. You don't want to break a bone and wind up getting carted outta here on a stretcher."

"Get off it. Skiing is the same as surfing. And I've been surfing for over a year."

"And you're good, but skiing is trickier. Water is softer than boulders."

"I don't see any boulders."

"This slope is groomed. But on the other courses you never know what's underneath the soft powder. It's just more dangerous. Trust me, especially the moguls."

"What are moguls?"

"Snow mounds, bumps. You jump from one to the next. It's crazy and real fast."

"I want to ski the moguls."

Exasperated, Sean looked at his watch, "Let's break for lunch and talk this out."

They leapt off the ski lift and skied down to the lodge. Seated outside on the deck, they were eating a nourishing soup and sipping hot chocolates while Sean did his best to convince Kathy to ski some intermediate slopes before tackling an expert run.

"Enough of this gibberish," Kathy said gruffly, "I want to ski the moguls, and I want longer skis."

"Come on Kathy, there's no sense rushing it. We could ski an expert run or, better yet, the giant slalom course. Work up to the moguls. They're brutally treacherous and worse than triple diamonds."

"Giant slalom; what's that?"

"A race course, but it's more forgiving than the moguls. Save those for another day."

"A race course, that sounds like fun, but I'll need longer skis, I want to keep up with you."

"Kathy, I don't want you getting injured."

"Look, Sean, I've been ice skating since I was a little girl."

"Yeah, I know. I'll never forget the time I saw you stick your leg over your head and spin around. That was sheer poetry in motion. But this is different, it's a long way to the bottom and nothing to grab onto."

Looking irritated, she growled, "Will you get me longer skis?"

"If you get hurt, I'm going to feel responsible."

"I don't tell you to slow down when you're drag racing or running with the football."

"Okay. But I'll have the technician set the bindings on the lowest setting."

"Why?"

"In case you fall, the skis are released from the bindings. It'll prevent you from breaking a leg."

When they finished their hot chocolates they went to rent longer skis. Against Sean's fervid advice, Kathy rented skis that came a foot over her head. After a couple of practice runs on the intermediate slopes, they skied off the chair lift over to the start of the giant slalom course and stared down as a cold, howling wind and a flurry of snow slapped their reddened faces.

"Yikes, you're right," said Kathy, covering her mouth with a furry mitten, "it is steep and almost straight down."

"You don't have to do this. I'm already impressed with how well you've been skiing."

She glared at Sean. "You think just because you're a guy, only guys can get airborne?"

"I don't think that, I just don't want you getting wiped out."

"I'm not a fraidy-cat, and I want to do this. I have confidence in my ability. You're always telling me how you thrive on competition. Well, so do I. Now let's ski."

"Hold on, Kathy. Man, you are stubborn. If you're so hell-bent, have it your way. It's fine with me. But will you please let me give you some helpful pointers before you wind up a cripple."

Kathy beamed. "Now let me find out how good of an instructor you are. Teach me to fly like a bird, mister teacher."

"Alright," he said, "but first, let me tell you what works for me. I ski like I'm on the Olympic ski team and winning the coveted gold medal; a world champion."

"That's the way I ice skate."

"I know. I've seen it in your face. But this is a whole different ballgame. Falling can be brutal punishment. Trust me; I've fallen halfway down this mountain. And it hurt."

Sean spent over an hour demonstrating the techniques his instructors had taught him when he was a little kid. He showed her how to shift her upper body, her hips, bend her knees in the tuck position, and planting the poles.

Looking exuberant, Kathy said, "I'm ready for the challenge to conquer this mountain, mister teacher."

"That's the spirit, my bold sweetheart. Be daring, but be cautious. One last important tip, don't cross your skis. Keep them pointed straight."

Sean took a deep breath and shook his head, watching Kathy bend her knees in the tuck position. With a fierce look of determination, she lowered her goggles, planted her poles and shoved off. Feeling proud, yet concerned for her welfare, he followed after Kathy, watching her zigzag undauntedly down the bending course. Amazed by her dexterity; Sean's heart thumped wildly as they raced down the straightaway. He tensed when he saw a small bump and watched Kathy soar in flight. While both of them were airborne, Sean grimaced when he turned and saw Kathy excitedly waving her ski poles with her ski tips crossed. Feeling panicky, he quickly braced himself and made a safe landing. Coming to an abrupt halt, Sean raised his goggles and watched Kathy plunging and tumbling down the slopes ski-less until she slammed into a small mound. He took a deep breath and raced to where she lay face down.

Kathy was sitting up, clutching her ribs and shaking her grimacing face when he got to her and unsnapped his bindings. He knelt beside her and said, "Good grief, that was some wicked fall. Are you okay?"

"I think my ribs may be broken or cracked," she screamed, "and my ankle hurts. Oh, my God, I can't stand the pain, I feel dizzy."

"I've got to get help. Don't move. I'll be right back."

Damn it, why wouldn't she listen to me? *Sean thought, planting his skis in the snow in the form of an X and began jumping, screaming and waving his poles like a maniac.*

Within a few minutes, a crowd of Samaritans skiers surrounded them. Seeing a ski patroller on a snowmobile racing towards him, Sean rushed back to Kathy and comforted her.

"Is the lady all right?" The ski patroller asked as he came to an abrupt halt.

"She thinks her ribs might be broken or cracked and maybe her ankle," replied Sean.

The ski patroller pulled out his mobile phone and called for aid. Shortly later, Kathy lay on a stretcher on the back of a snowmobile. Sean could hear her screaming as he skied behind the snowmobile, feeling guilty. *You warned her. She wouldn't listen. It's not your fault. She's too darn mule-headed.*

In was late in the afternoon and Sean was nervously pacing inside the emergency waiting room at the Tahoe Forest Hospital in Truckee. A young nurse came into the waiting room holding some X-rays and she hurried over to Sean.

"Your friend is a lucky girl," said the nurse as Kathy hobbled into the room with the aid of crutches and a painful expression, "the X-rays show that two of her ribs are only slightly fractured and her ankle is a minor sprain."

Shaking his head, Sean clasped Kathy's hand and said to the nurse, "Thank you for the good news. I've been worried sick."

The nurse looked at Sean and said, "She's young and will heal easily in two to four weeks." The nurse turned to Kathy and handed her a small bag. "There is ample pain medication inside until you have your prescription filled at your local pharmacy."

"Thank you," said Kathy.

"Good luck to you," said the nurse before she turned and walked away.

"Whatever you do, Sean," said Kathy, "don't make me laugh, it hurts."

"I know, I've cracked a couple of ribs a few times," he said. "It's painful. My heart goes out to you."

"I was flying like a bird until my skis crossed."

"I saw that," he said. "It freaked me out. I'm sure glad you're okay."

"I coughed a little while ago and thought I'd die. But the shot they gave me is beginning to kick in. I can't wait to do that again."

"After that hair-raising fall, are you nuts? I thought this would teach you a lesson."

"Will you stop badgering me? I'm not a quitter."

"You're a glutton for punishment. We have to hustle before it starts snowing and I have to put on chains."

"Why?"

"For traction, driving on black ice is dangerous. Man, your dad is going to be peeved when he sees those crutches."

The paperwork signed and Kathy's rental skis returned; they drove halfway down the mountain, arguing about patience before their conversation started mellowing out.

*   *   *

Kathy had fully recovered when high school was coming to a close. On a spring afternoon, Sean drove into the Shell gas station where Sal worked.

"Another gas war," said Sean, taking off the gas cap. "You can't beat 13 cents, filler up with super pal. Then get the windows, check the tires, oil and water. And don't forget the battery."

Sal laughed. "Buzz off. So ya finally beat *FireEater*," he said, pulling off the hose and pumping the gas. "That was one hell of a close race the other night."

"Yeah, *Lil Reb* was running at peak perfection. I wouldn't have had a chance against him if it hadn't been for you helping me mount that supercharger. Thanks big time."

"No sweat," said Sal.

"He still disputes that call," said Sean. "Damn guy protested, cussing and kicking gravel at the finish line, yelling he had me beat by a half a fender."

"I saw him," said Sal. "Arnie totally flipped out. I laughed my butt off. Never saw him have a temper tantrum before."

"Neither had I. Oh, well, he'll get over it. Having the reputation of having the fastest car has created some havoc I never counted on."

"Why's that?"

"Every time I go out with Kathy and we're cruising on El Camino," said Sean, "I'm being harassed at every red light by some speed demon. It's hard to decline the challenge. Speed's contagious enough."

"I know what you mean," said Sal. "I've got to cool it myself. Cops nabbed me the other night. Some jerk revved his engine and then stared at me like he was a hot shot. What really ticked me off was when he furrowed his brow and squinted at me like he was a tough guy. That really peeved me."

"I'll bet."

"Anyway, I left the jerk at the intersection like he was standing still. Then I see flashing red lights. Man, the cop who pulled me over went ape shit. He thought I was drunk or high on some drug. I told him I didn't drink or do drugs, but he made me walk the line anyway. I passed the test, but the dork gave me a ticket for doing ninety in a thirty-five."

"Wow," said Sean. "I'm surprised the DMV hasn't yanked your driver's license yet."

"I've got a hearing coming up next month."

"You're kidding me, so do I," said Sean. "That gives us some time to figure out a plan. We'll come up with something. On top of all the speeding tickets, I got two tickets for excessive noise and one for exhibition of speed, spinning rubber. I'm telling them I'm seeing a shrink."

"That's a heck of a good idea," said Sal. "I think I'll tell them the same thing. It means we're seeking help because we have a compulsion for speed."

"With a little luck, it might just work," said Sean. "Hey, do you think your older brother could pick me up a pint of apricot brandy for the senior ball?"

"Sure, same stuff as the junior prom?"

"Yeah, Kathy loved it. She said it went down smooth. I'm hoping to loosen her up, you know, lower her inhibitions. God, do I want to unsnap her bra."

Sal hung the gas pump on the tank and twisted the gas cap back on. "You haven't gone that far yet?"

Sean shrugged and handed Sal a five spot.

"Man, you are slow," said Sal.

"Hey Sal, what about the windows and tires?"

Sal handed Sean his change. "That's for customers. I ain't your slave. Check 'em yourself."

On the night of the senior ball, Sean stepped into the foyer at Kathy's house spiffed up in a tailed, black tuxedo, with a frilly white shirt, bow tie, suspenders and a red cummerbund. A pink carnation was pinned to his lapel and he carried a fancy black and silver cane, and a corsage of purple orchids.

"Don't you look dashing this evening," said Carl.

"Thank you."

"Come into the study and let me mix you a Rob Roy while you're waiting for Kathy. Big night like this, she'll be lollygagging awhile and those flowers in your hand will have started to wilt."

Stirring his drink, Sean sat chatting with Carl about sports. A half hour had passed when Kathy finally made her grand entrance. She stood posing at the doorway, twirling her golden locks. Sean's eyes almost popped out of their sockets when he saw her bulging cleavage and tipped his black top hat. "You are something to behold," he said.

"Thank you," she said, sashaying sexily across the room over to Sean. "You look pretty dapper yourself."

Carl grabbed his light meter and camera. "You two lovebirds get up the stairs and say cheese."

Sean and Kathy bounded up the stairs. Standing beside Kathy on the upstairs landing and nearly speechless, Sean did a double take and managed to say, "Wow, I don't believe you. What a transformation. You look the most beautiful I've ever seen you, like a full-grown woman."

"Don't rush me," she said, "I'm not ready. I still prefer being a girl. But look at you, Prince Charming. You look so debonair, so gallant."

"Enough swooning," Carl called out. "Stand at the rail and Sean, pin that corsage on Kathy's gown."

Sean took his eyes off Kathy's cleavage and looked at her sparkling eyes. "Ah, this thing is pretty sharp. I don't want to stick you by accident."

"You can do it."

Kathy was overflowing with bubbles as Sean nervously pinned the corsage on the lavender upper folds of her gown and they wrapped their arms around each other's waists. She looked radiant standing at his side as he stared at her breasts.

"Look at the camera, Sean."

Embarrassed, Sean's eyes quickly raised to Kathy's enchanting eyes.

Finished posing for Carl, they pranced down the stairs and Kathy grabbed a purple shawl from off a hook.

"You two make a charming couple," said Carl. "Remember, Kathy, two-o-clock sharp."

"The Tonga room closes at two," said Sean. "Afterwards, everyone's going to Mel's Diner for root beer floats. Couldn't you make it two thirty, pretty please?"

"Alright," said Carl, rubbing his jaw, "but not a minute later."

Kathy beamed. "Thanks, Dad,"

"You sure look terrific," said Sean as they stepped outside and Carl closed the front door.

"Oh goodie, the top's up, how sweet of you to remember."

"Isn't that what knights in shining armor do? Sean said. "If it starts to rain, I'll take off my coat and lay it in front of your feet."

She smiled. "You can't imagine the pain in the behind it is having long hair. It takes me hours to get out all the knots and tangles when you have the top down."

"My sister complains about the same thing," said Sean, opening the car door for Kathy."

Holding the corsage to her nose, she said, "Thank you for the orchids, they smell delightful, and match my shawl."

Seated behind the wheel, Sean started the engine and they headed to the Fairmont Hotel atop Nob Hill in San Francisco, talking about what they would have for dinner.

"I feel in the mood for something exotic," said Kathy. "Isn't The Tonga Room Hawaiian?"

"I think so, but I'm not sure. I've never had Hawaiian food. Have you?"

"No, it's too fattening," she replied. "It's nothing but blubber. I'd prefer eating the apples, pineapples, papayas and mangos that the Hawaiians stuff in the pigs mouths."

As hard as he tried, Sean couldn't keep from peeking at Kathy's cleavage and hearing her say the words papayas and mangos made it even worse.

"I like things that are sweet, succulent, and tender, as long as it's not fattening," she said. "You're weaving," she screamed. "Will you please pay attention to the darn road."

On the verge of having a fit, Sean swerved back into his lane. "I'm under control. Just a slight diversion, but I'm okay."

"Maybe I should sit away from you so you can concentrate on driving."

"Naw, you're fine. It was just a little lapse."

"Would you mind taking your eyes off my boobs, it's bugging me. Or do you want me to put on my shawl?"

"Then stop talking about juicy, sweet and succulent."

She laughed. "I'm sorry."

Parking the car in the underground garage below the Fairmont Hotel, Sean said, "Feel in the mood for a little eye opener to sort of loosen up the inner spirits?"

"Sure," she said. "Did you get the apricot brandy?"

He grinned. "Yeah."

They each took a healthy swig from his father's silver flask and scrunched their faces. A few minutes later, they were swinging arms and staring at the chandeliers as they crossed the lobby to the glass elevator. The Tonga Room was packed with a horde of rambunctious seniors dressed like royalty when they walked inside. They headed straight to the buffet table and Sean filled two glasses from the punch bowl. Sipping umbrella drinks, they roamed from table to table mingling with friends as Sean scanned the crowd in search of Sal and Arnie. Sean spotted Marylou and Caroline, eagerly waving at him. Everyone at the lavishly decorated table greeted Sean and Kathy with hearty embraces.

"What the hell took you two so long?" said Arnie. "Grab a table and slide it over."

While the guys joined two tables together, Kathy rushed off to the girl's bathroom with Caroline and Marylou.

"Man this place is tit city," said Sean. "Every chick in here is wearing a push-up bra. I've never seen so many plunging necklines."

"It's better than being at the beach," said Sal. "Wait till you see Wanda Skaggs. Her boobies are ready to burst the seams of her dress."

"What say we have a toast with a shot of tequila and kick this celebration into high gear?" Arnie said.

The three boys stopped talking about their planned upcoming jaunt across the country after graduation when they saw the girls coming back to the table, giggling and glowing. Sal's girlfriend Marylou, usually soft-spoken, was in high spirits, looking hot in a low-cut sequined dark blue evening gown. Arnie's gal, Caroline, always cheerful and a lusty-eyed charmer, sat poised at the festive table like a statuesque model, polite and attentive in her bright red evening gown. Everyone kept sneaking their tropical umbrella drinks under the table and adding brandy and tequila to them while keeping a close eye on the staff. They all slyly brought up their glasses, stirred their drinks and toasted to anything and everything. Waiters and waitresses, carrying silver trays over their heads with one hand, laid out a smorgasbord of sumptuous appetizers. Sean ordered what everyone at the table ordered, Hawaiian spare ribs. Kathy ordered a lean filet mignon.

After dinner and socializing, Kathy and Sean shifted to a smaller candlelit table for two.

"It's nice being alone with you," said Sean.

"I feel the same way," she said, gently squeezing his hand. "I like hanging out with our friends, but the ambiance is much more romantic here. You should see the candle flames dancing on your eyes. You look so handsome tonight in that tuxedo."

Sean stared at her, entranced. "And you should see the prisms of light flickering and bouncing off that tiara on your head. I love your dress and the way your eyes are sparkling. You look so exquisite, so natural and so delicate. You are a certified, one hundred percent quintessential beauty."

She stared at him, spellbound. "Those are the most precious words you have ever spoken to me." She squeezed his hand harder. "That's why I'm so madly in love with you."

"Love: that sure was a tough word for me to get out. Now, it flows out like it's coated in baby oil."

Sean had a vision of Kathy's body coated in shiny oil as they sat dreamy-eyed, staring at each other and saying sweet words until the music beckoned them to shake, rattle and roll on the dance floor. It helped that they were both feeling a little tipsy when the band played the Rumba and then the Mambo. The brandy especially helped loosen their joints when the orchestra started playing the Cha-cha. Kathy was all over the dance floor. One moment she was dancing up a storm, the next she was flirting like a seductive enchantress. Her cerulean eyes glittered like sprinkled stardust as he twirled her around. With a tantalizing smile, they went back to the table and Kathy took off her stiletto, high-heel shoes and slipped on a pair of dance slippers over her nylon stocking feet. Sean shook his head watching her sashay back onto the dance floor, his eyes shifted to her slender waist and the way the fluted gown clung tightly to her rounded hips. So aroused, his imagination stripped her naked. Half delirious, he spun her again and the two crashed into each other, tumbling to the floor. Sitting cross-legged, the center of attention, they broke out in laughter.

"Are you okay, Kathy?" Scott Simpson asked, extending his hand. "You're sweating profusely."

Sean sprang to his feet and raised his fists. "Look, Scott, I don't know what your game is but I've had it with you. Do you hear me?"

With a spiteful grin, Scott said, "Loud and clear, just offering to help the lady."

"Over my dead body."

"That might just be the case."

Kathy stood up on her own and grabbed Sean's arms. "Please Sean, it's the senior Ball. It's an oven in here," she said, "I need some fresh air."

"So do I, let's take a walk outside."

Sean kept a close eye on Scott as he walked over to join his two cronies and their pathetic looking dates at a table while Kathy put on her shawl. Outside in the cool breeze, Sean and Kathy watched the cable cars, and listened to the clanging bells.

"You seem so quiet all of a sudden," said Kathy.

"I don't know why that chump has it out for me. I feel like going back in and kicking that guy's butt, but another part of me wants to be alone with you. I'm having too much fun being with you to let that creep louse up the night."

"Forget that loser."

"You're right.

"We could leave, if you'd like. I mean after we say goodbye to everyone."

"I was thinking we could take a stroll on the beach. Maybe catch a shooting star or some galactic nebula."

Kathy beamed. "I'd like that."

The music had toned down when they went back inside the Tonga Room and began swaying their bodies in sync to the music under the dim lights.

"Sal and Marylou look to be madly in love," said Kathy.

Sean grinned when saw Arnie and Caroline entangled in a spastic seizure of hand groping. "Everyone in here seems to be in love."

Kathy stopped dancing and stared at him, "I feel woozy, let's leave," she whispered.

His eyes glinted when he heard Kathy say the word woozy. Her lucid eyes seemingly calling out, Take me, I'm yours. After saying goodbyes to their friends, Sean's heart began throbbing so fast that his equilibrium nearly faltered as they wobbled into the elevator. They both tripped and stumbled out of the elevator into the lobby. Inside the parking garage, they staggered arm in arm to the car while laughing.

A half hour later, they sat cuddled tightly together in a romantic tryst parked atop a bluff overlooking the Pacific Ocean. Wolfman Jack howled and played a soft love ballad on the radio.

"You can put the top down if you want," she said. "The wind has died. It's turned out to be such a lovely night and I want to see the stars twinkle. There's a myriad of stars tonight."

"You're sure you won't be too cold?"

"I have my wool shawl."

Sean put the top down, and slid next to Kathy, sliding his arm over her bare shoulders.

"Wow, did you see that?" Kathy said excitedly.

Staring at her luscious breasts, Sean said, "No, where? What was it?"

"A brilliant shooting star," she said. "It just streaked across the sky and fizzled out."

"I must have blinked, I missed it."

"Don't worry," she said, "there'll be plenty more. There must be a zillion stars in the sky tonight."

They were stargazing when a chilly wind from the sea swept over them, causing Kathy to shiver and forcing Sean to put the top back up. He fired the engine and turned on the heater. Within minutes the windows were steamy as their body temperatures rose to a fever from all their lubricious caressing, licking and nibbling.

In the midst of their heated passion, Sean was snapped out of his reverie when Kathy shoved him away.

"Stop it, Sean," she scowled, "let's not get nasty. You have to learn to control yourself."

"Me?" Sean said, sitting up. "What about you? You're the one who dragged me on top of you. You're the one who's been tantalizing me all night, getting me all worked up. Now you tell me to stop and expect me to control myself just like that, in an instant. I don't have your self-control. My hormones are raging."

She abruptly jerked up and started adjusting her clothes. "You're right. I guess I have been teasing you. I'm sorry, but I have cravings too. You really turn me on. I want to do the nasty just as badly as you do."

"See, there you go again," Sean gruffed. "What's with this nasty stuff? What's nasty? There's nothing nasty about sex. You have a hang-up with sex. Let's not get naughty, Sean," he mimicked her. "Let's not get vulgar. Let's not get dirty. I need air. This car is a damn sweat box." He opened the door. "These escapades are driving me insane."

Sean quickly exited the car and started walking down a narrow path to the beach. Kathy put on her shawl and hurriedly followed after him. She caught up with him, flung her arm around him and kissed him.

"I'm sorry," she said as they walked slowly. "I just can't have sex now." She paused and took a deep breath. "I'm not ready to have a baby. Please forgive me?"

Sean stopped walking and turned to face her. "Yeah, sure. I'm sorry too. It's just, you know . . . it's becoming almost impossible to suppress these urges I feel. I've been whacked out of my mind all night looking at you wiggle your fanny and flaunt your breasts."

"I would love to let you play with them, but that would lead to. Oh, Sean, we both need to cool off." She slipped her hand into his.

"Hey, Angel Eyes, I'm sorry for getting carried away like that. You just have a way of getting me so aroused that I lose control of myself."

"How do you think I feel? And for your information, I don't have any hang-ups about sex. I am not frigid."

"I know that. It was a dumb thing for me to say. I said it out of frustration. I didn't mean it. I guess it's good that you're so level-headed."

"It's not easy, because . . . I have a strong desire to make love with you."

"Really?" He looked surprised as they began walking. "You mean all the way?"

"Now who's the one acting dumb? Yes, really. Lust is innate in everyone."

Sean flinched. "Wow! I like it when you talk like that. Do you ever have fantasies about us having sex?"

"You'd better believe it," she said, "all the time. They can sometimes be overpowering. Our sexual desires are equal. It's just that women tend to be less aggressive than men. Right now, I'm just as horny as you are. My whole body itches and tingles."

Sean shook his head and they broke into a fit of laughter. "It's a breakthrough," he said, "a revelation, you fantasizing about sex. Have you ever had a wet dream?"

Looking flustered, she sputtered, "Women don't have wet dreams, silly."

"I meant have you ever, ah, you know, ah, masturbated?"

"That's personal. How about you, have you?"

"Ah, well, a few times. Now it's your turn. One secret for another."

"No. Well, not exactly."

Sean stopped walking and looked closely at Kathy. "What do you mean, not exactly?"

"What do you think; that only boys have all the fun?"

"You've masturbated?"

Kathy answered cautiously. "That's a very personal question." She paused in reflection. "In keeping our relationship honest, I have on occasion; mostly experimenting."

Blown away, Sean asked, "Have you ever had a climax?"

"I'm not sure."

"Oh, Kathy," he said, lifting her up and swinging her around. "When you do, you'll be in for a whopping surprise."

When they finished laughing, Sean asked, "Want to go to the Santa Cruz boardwalk tomorrow?"

"I would go anywhere with you. I love you."

"I love you too. You make my heart go zing."

"Next week, let's malinger and play hooky and go to the KPIX dance party."

"Groovy."

On the beach Kathy unsnapped her nylons from her garter belt, kicked off her high heels, and held up the hem of her gown. Sean followed suit and rolled his trousers up to his knees. The starry-eyed couple strolled barefoot along the wet sand, splashing through the foamy surf, and listening to the waves crashing.

"Why are you laughing?" Kathy asked.

"You and I talking like this, about sex, masturbation, having climaxes and such, and it all sounds so natural."

Kathy smiled and blushed, her eyes twinkling from the light of the moon. He took out a handkerchief and wiped her eyelashes.

"You know, you don't need to use makeup and all this stuff," Sean said dreamily. "You're a natural beauty, a work of art, a masterpiece."

"You're a fickle one," Kathy responded. "I only use it for a little enhancement."

"Believe me; you don't need any artificial enhancers. Anyway, I'm glad we didn't take a limo like most of the other kids. What would we do in the backseat with a chauffer sitting in the front, watching us in the rearview mirror?"

Kathy stared at him quizzically then looked in the direction of Venus, flickering brightly in the dark southern sky. "If you promise not to go any further, you can do anything you want with my boobs and behind, but nothing else."

Sean's eyes lit up. "I promise."

At exactly two thirty with a half moon encircled by a golden nimbus over their heads, they tiptoed up the stairs to the porch and embraced. Feeling frustrated, perplexed and hornier than he had ever felt, Sean drove home.

Lying in bed, he slowly masturbated while recalling how Kathy's body twitched while he suckled her nipples and rubbed her fanny.

9

COMMENCEMENT DAY CAME with a sonic boom in early June of '62, when Sean and Kathy strolled into the jam-packed high school auditorium. Like the rest of their classmates, they were wearing floor length black robes and mortarboard caps, with jiggling golden tassels. Smirking wildly, they excitedly traipsed up and down the aisles, shaking hands, backslapping and jabbering with their fellow peers. A hoarse voice blared over the loud speakers, telling the reveling crowd to please take a seat.

When the senior graduation class was seated and anxiously awaiting their turn to march down the aisle, Principal Langostini laggardly walked across the stage to the podium. He spread out a sheet of paper and began reciting in a throaty voice.

Almost an hour later, Sean jolted in his seat when he heard the Principal call out his name and a proud grin appeared on his face. Feeling confident he would conquer the world, Sean sprang out of his seat and coolly strutted down the center aisle. A warm smile appeared on old Langostini's pudgy, round face when he shook Sean's hand. Sean snatched his diploma, somersaulted across the stage and back flipped onto the carpet. Beaming proudly, he raised the diploma over his head and traipsed to his seat, flapping his arms like a bird.

Twenty minutes later, Sean blew Kathy a kiss as she loftily glided back up the aisle, shining like a supernova and waving her diploma.

At the conclusion of the ceremony, Sean stood beside Kathy as they thrust their fists into the air and both shouted, "Yahoo! We did it!" Sean turned to Kathy and said, "There's been so much going on these past few days I forgot to tell you. My folks told me that somebody from Stanford called. I might be getting a scholarship there."

"Huh," Kathy said, squirming and looking disappointed.

"What's with the sudden look of gloomy doom? Is something wrong?"

"It's just that it's so far away," she said with a sullen expression. "I'll be in Michigan."

"Maybe Michigan State will call. Anyway, if Stanford's interested in me other schools must be. Let's talk about it later. It's time to party."

"Don't mind me," she said with a bubbly smile, "go where you want, Stanford's tops."

"Who cares, I want to be with my gal."

"Come on," she said, taking his hand, "my father wants to take pictures and I want to meet your family."

"Not too long," said Sean. "I'm in the mood to celebrate. It's a day of jubilation. 12 years of cracking the books is a long time."

The remainder of the morning went by in a high-speed blur as Sean and Kathy posed for their parents and relatives, varying their postures and smiling until their faces began hurting. The fact that Sean's parents and Kathy's father and his blond bombshell fiancé were getting along so well was a huge relief for Sean. Seeing Kathy smiling happily with his family, a large weight was lifted from Sean's shoulders.

After socializing with family and relatives, Kathy and Sean roamed around the bustling auditorium, autographing yearbooks. Sean got a kick every time he signed the picture of Kathy and him in the yearbook, proclaiming them to be the couple most likely to get hitched.

"Let's hit the beach," said Arnie.

"What are we waiting for," said Sal. "Surf's up, it's time for some heavenly bliss."

"Then let's boogie," said Sean, turning to Kathy. "I'll pick you up in an hour at your pad."

Finished chatting with his family and relatives at his house, Sean changed into baggy madras shorts and a T-shirt. He grabbed the bags he had packed the night before and ran to the garage. Grabbing his surfboard, he lashed it in the backseat, and drove to Kathy's house. She came skipping out of the garage barefoot, licking a lollipop, swinging a tote bag and wearing a loose fitting blouse and frayed cut-off jeans. Her hair was braided in pigtails with pink ribbons tied in bows.

"Will you get my board," said Kathy. "It's in the garage."

"Sure."

With Kathy's surfboard tied and sticking out of the back seat alongside of Sean's, the radio turned up almost full-blast, and the Beach Boys singing *Good Vibrations,* Sean drove to Rockaway Beach.

After Sean parked on top of a steep cliff, they lugged their surfboards and carefully trudged down a winding path. Reaching the beach, they sprinted merrily to where their fellow graduates were stacking timber for the sunset bonfire. Still grinning and laughing from the day's excitement, they dug their surfboards into the warm sand. Being part of the volunteer bonfire brigade, they each grabbed a sled and set out across the beach scavenging firewood. Sandy Cliffhouse and his band, *The Velveteens* were setting up generators, amplifiers, and large speakers on a wooden stage. Sandy was the guy who had driven the getaway car on the morning Sean and Arnie heisted Judge Tommason's hubcaps.

Sal and Marylou, part of the refreshment crew, were carrying cases of beer and stashing them under a concession stand. Arnie and Caroline were emptying sacks of ice into washtubs and barrels that were filled with cans of Bud, Coors and Rainier Ale. Sean and Kathy continued to pitch in, hauling logs, branches and anything combustible until the huge stack resembled a giant pyramid.

By mid-afternoon the scorching sun turned the sand hot and Sandy and *The Velveteens* were cranking out rock and roll on the small stage. Along with everyone else, Sean and Kathy shed their clothing down to their bathing suits. Kathy's new skimpy bikini caused Sean to momentarily gape before they streaked across the frothy sand and dove into the freezing Pacific Ocean. They came out covered in goose bumps and shivering as kids were dancing the bop to rock and roll and girls were swiveling hula-hoops on their hips.

The more the quicksilver heated up, the more Sandy and his band got revved up.

"Your friend Sandy is something else," said Kathy as they danced. "I've never seen anyone leap about like he does. He really gets fired up."

"Yeah, he's going to make the big time. Sandy and his band just got back from recording a demo album in Hollywood. Some producer down in LA is working on cuttin' a deal with a record label."

"How cool," she said and swilled a mouthful of beer.

Sandy's entire torso was lathered in sweat when he ripped the red silk shirt off his back, leaving his skinny body naked except for the skintight, black leather pants and bright orange scarf wrapped around his neck. The scarf flowed down his freckled, pale white skin to his bare feet. Other than Sean's dad's beatnik friends, Sandy was one of the few young people Sean had ever seen whose flaming red hair fell past his shoulders.

"Yeah," said Kathy, "Sandy's one heck of a performer. There's something unique about his voice too. I've a strong hunch he's going to be a famous rock star after his album's released."

"That's for sure. He's a heck of a songwriter too."

"I know," said Kathy, "I love his lyrics."

Up on the stage in a wet fever, Sandy looped the microphone, pranced and fell into the splits. He sprang up and back-flipped onto the sand and deftly bounced back up onto the stage. Singing one of his compositions, *Shaking under the California Sun*, Sandy flung the microphone over his head and between his legs, whirling it in arcing circles. At the end of the song, he hurled the microphone from the stage and ran back to bang on the keys while a roadie plugged in another microphone and Sandy belted *Teeny Weenie Polka Dot Bikini*.

Sitting on the sand, drinking beer and watching Sandy perform, Sean slid his arm around Kathy's bare waist and reflected back on the nights Sandy, Arnie, and Sal came to his house for boogie-woogie jam sessions with his dad. He told Kathy about the times Sandy banged the ivory and ebony keys of his electric piano, wailing up a storm while his father picked the strings of an electric guitar and blew into a harmonica.

"What about you, Sal and Arnie?" Kathy asked Sean, "Are you guys going to join in?"

"Yeah, later," said Sean. "We're gonna rip this place apart."

"Sal's incredible on the timbale," said Kathy. "When he gets in sync, his fingers move in a blur."

"Yeah," said Sean, "and Arnie kicks butt on base guitar."

"You three sing darn good background vocals too. Did you bring your tambourine?"

"You bet," said Sean, "we're going to get down and crank out some surfer rock later tonight. Right now it's time to be jolly." He looked her up and down. "I really like your new bathing suit."

"It's too revealing. It makes me feel uncomfortable. And I don't want you getting all excited."

"You could be wearing a muumuu and I'd still be charged-up. Hey, they're setting up a limbo pole. Come on, I wanna watch you shimmy when the pole gets real low."

"Get off your duffs you two and let's ride some curls," Arnie yelled as he and Caroline jogged passed them with their surfboards tucked under their arms.

"Come on," hollered Caroline, let's groove in the tube."

"Hey, buster," Kathy scowled as Arnie and Caroline splashed across the shoreline, "what in the dickens were you doing staring Caroline's boobs?"

Sean grinned. "What are you talking about?"

"Don't give me that dumb, innocent look," she said in a harsh voice. "You were doing more than staring, that was more like gawking or ogling. Your tongue was half out of your mouth."

"Okay, so I looked. There's no harm in looking."

"How would you feel if you saw me staring at the front of a guy's bulging bathing suit?"

"Okay, you're right. But it's strictly instinct. What was I supposed to do, turn around and cover my eyes? No need for you to go berserk. She's always flaunting her boobies."

"Yuck, they're gross," said Kathy. "I can't understand what guys see in big boobs like that. They'll be sagging down to her belly button after she has her first baby."

"Hey, Angel Eyes," he said, putting his arm around her and pulling her beside him. "It's you I'm mad about. You're my gal. Come on, thaw out. Surfs up, let's catch some thrills. You can do the limbo pole after we ride a couple of waves"

Kathy and Caroline were among the elite handful of girls at school who possessed the intrepid daring and agility to hang ten. Marylou was content to lie on a beach towel and watch Sal wax his board while she rubbed suntan lotion on her dark skinned body. Loaded with paranoid phobias, Marylou was afraid to wade out any further than her knees. She was always harping about undertow, sharks, and other creatures that lurked in the ocean.

Kathy and Caroline were good buddies but when it came to surfing, they were fiercely competitive. As they honed their skills, riding in the groove and cutting back over the crest became a natural high for them. It also boosted Sean and Arnie's egos, knowing they were their gals.

"Let's ride the waves," Sal called out, running past Kathy and Sean with his surfboard."

Kathy and Sean grabbed their boards and ran splashing through the choppy waves. Past the breakers, they paddled out with Sal to wait with Arnie and Caroline for the monster wave.

"Check out the size of that swell," said Caroline, "that's going to be a killer ride."

"It's the bombora," shouted Kathy.

As the rising hump of ocean swept past them, Kathy and Caroline began frantically paddling. They stood up on their boards and bent forward, each dipping a hand in water. The two girls displayed their incredible balance and coordination, riding on the crest and then disappeared into the tube.

"Ain't they something to behold," said Sean.

"Yeah, two brave hearts," said Arnie.

"If surfing was an Olympic event," said Sean, "Kathy would easily win a gold medal."

"I'm not sure Caroline would be willing to settle for silver," said Arnie.

Sal pointed. "Looks like a tidal wave brewing."

"You tell Kathy about the road trip?" Arnie asked Sean.

"Haven't had the guts," he replied. "She keeps talking about all the plans she's made for us, things we're gonna do together this summer. I don't know what to say to her. I suspect she's gonna be real pissed off when I do tell her. But I'm going to; that's for sure."

"How about you, Sal," Arnie said. "You tell Marylou?"

"I'm kinda like Sean," said Sal. "I haven't got up the nerve to tell Marylou. How 'bout you?"

"Caroline wasn't exactly jumping with joy," said Arnie, but she said it'd be okay."

Sean slapped the water. "Darn, you told Caroline were going?"

"What's the big deal?" Arnie said.

"Gees, Arnie," said Sean, "you know how girls love to gossip. They're probably yakking about it right now."

"Sean's right, Arnie, Sal blurted."

"For crying out loud, I know that," said Arnie. "That's why I told Caroline not to mention it. She's cool and can keep a secret." He turned, his eyes wide open, "You two feeling the surge of that swell? "She looks to be powerful. You were right, Sal, this might be a killer breaker."

"What are you two kahunas waiting for," shouted Sean. "Let's ride that avalanche."

The three boys paddled like mad dogs and stood up as they skimmed along the hump. Bending their bodies low, they shot into a long greenish blue funnel. Filled with exhilaration, the boys blasted out of the tube, riding the wave to shore.

"Man, that was some incredible ride," said Sean as the three trudged onto the beach, "and none of us wiped out."

"We're kahunas," said Sal.

"This party's jamming," said Arnie.

"You'd best anoint yourself with some suntan oil," Sal told Sean, "you're almost beet red."

"I'm going to," said Sean, looking over at the beach volley game. "I'll be a son of a gun," he said angrily, "it's that chump, Scott Simpson, staring at Kathy's boobs with his tongue sticking out. It fries my ass."

"I wouldn't worry about it," said Arnie. "That jerk's headed to the joint."

"Arnie's right," said Sal. "You seen the dog meat that punk's here with."

"Yeah, that chick's gross," said Sean, "but it still gripes me to no end the way the prick is always staring at Kathy. I feel like smashing his face to a pulp."

"I wouldn't sweat it," said Arnie, "Kathy's hot for you."

"Besides, Sean," said Sal, "all three of us are lucky guys. Those are our gals jumping up and down with their bronzed bodies glimmering under the bright sun. They're the finest babes on the beach."

"You're right, Sal," said Sean. "Let's play volleyball."

Sean merely flicked Scott Simpson a surly grin and flipped him the bird in passing him to join the game.

Just as the golden sun was dipping towards the horizon, the crowd of revelers sat on the sand waiting for the green flash.

"What is a green flash?" Kathy asked.

"You've never seen one?" Sean replied.

"No."

"You're in for a real treat," he said, "It's like a mirage, only it's not an illusion. When it starts, try not to blink or you might miss it. They're real fast and spiffy."

"What happens?"

"You'll see," he said. "It's a phenomena."

"What causes it?"

"Something to do with refraction," he said.

The roar from the crowd was near deafening when the sun touched down on the horizon and the sky turned reddish orange. In an instant, a brilliant, fiery green flash streaked along the horizon and the class of '62 went bonkers.

"That was so cool," said Kathy. "The sky was on fire."

"It's an omen that this is going to be a night to remember," said Sean. "The human pyramid is next."

When gloaming twilight came and a cool breeze blew in from the sea, Sean finally felt the jealous tension ease, when he watched Kathy wrap her body in clothing.

"Higher-higher-higher," the torch bearing revelers cried out as the human pyramid began to rise. Kathy winked at Sean when he hefted her on top of his shoulders, gripping her calves tightly as she struggled to maintain her balance at the top of the five body high pyramid. The pyramid wobbled and seemed on the verge of toppling, but the strongmen at the base held steadfast.

The crowd cheered as chunks of driftwood were being passed up. As the pile of timber rose higher, a small cedar box with a cryptic message was passed up. Kathy had been granted the honor of placing it on top of the bonfire. As she set the box inside a wooden crate, the strongmen below began laughing and the almost thirty foot high pyramid teetered. Sean clutched Kathy's shaky calves tighter as bodies wavered.

"Jump Kathy," Sean yelled. "Jump as far as you can. This thing's going down."

Amidst the frightened yelling, Kathy and Sean leapt just as the pyramid tottered and collapsed. They landed on their feet and fell forward with their faces in the sand. Laughing hysterically, they looked at the crumpled bodies crawling around, amazed that everyone was laughing and no one was screaming.

"It's a miracle no one got hurt," said Kathy with an astonished expression.

"Must be the booze," said Sean.

Wanda Skaggs, the high school homecoming queen, licked her lips before she touched a burning torch to the kindling at the base of the huge stack of timber. Moments later, the bonfire was ablaze and flames were streaking thirty and forty feet high, sizzling and fizzling into the black sky. As the heat grew more intense, the tipsy crowd of graduates staggered back fifty-feet and formed a ring around the bonfire.

"This is totally awesome," Kathy slurred rhapsodically, looking giddy and flushed. She belched and said, "It reminds me of a burning temple."

"Like a Mayan sacrificial burial where virgins were burned alive to appease the gods," said Sal.

Arnie hiccupped and popped open a can of beer with a church key. "I read somewhere that the Mayan warriors cut out the hearts from virgins and ate 'em raw."

"Ugh! I know," Caroline said. "How grotesque, and they drank the blood. It gives me the creepy crawlers just thinking about it."

Grinning, Sal looked at Kathy. "The Scandinavians still do it, mostly the Norwegians," he said teasingly.

"No they don't," Kathy angrily slurred, glaring at Sal. "That's a lie."

Sal raised his flask, took a swig and furled his brow. "They sure as heck do," he said, "maybe not virgins but deer. I read an article in *National Geographic* with a picture a Norwegian guy slitting a reindeer's jugular. Blood was squirting into the big stein he held."

"That's not true," shouted Kathy.

"Sure is," said Sal. "There was another picture showing the guy glugging it down. Blood was splattered all over his face. Talk about grisly."

"How gross," said Marylou.

"That's a filthy lie you disgusting pig," Kathy spouted at Sal and turned away.

"I don't believe you," Caroline challenged. "You're just making that up to hurt Kathy's feelings."

Sal crossed his heart and said, "It's the truth, I swear to God and hope to die. The article said the Norwegians think it's a magic potion that makes you younger."

Kathy sneered at Sal. "Your mind's warped."

"Anyway, look at the bright side, Kathy," said Arnie, "at least it's only the blood of a reindeer and not the blood of a young, innocent virgin girl."

"Come on, Sean," said Kathy, "let's shake rattle and roll."

"That away, Kathy," Arnie said. "It's time to get down and celebrate this commemoration."

At midnight, Arnie, Sal, and Sean joined Sandy and *The Velveteens* on the stage, belting out, *Rockin' on the Beach*.

Several songs later, they toned down the tempo with one of Sandy's romantic ballads, *Moon Praising* and young lovers began drifting along the sand arm in arm, vanishing into the misty night fog. When Sandy began playing his latest composition, *Empyrean Angel*, Sean took Kathy's hand and the lovebirds disappeared into the dark, carrying a double-sized sleeping bag and a pup tent.

Embraced inside the small dark tent making-out and engaged in passionate body exploration, their kisses became more slobbering and their tongues probed deeper than they ever had. At first, Sean thought it was the chill of the night air flowing through the zipper of the sleeping bag that caused Kathy to slacken her usual defense system. It surprised him even more that she wasn't resisting. The urgency in her body movements had him wishing he could see her. She wasn't whispering a hushed no or telling him to stop, and she wasn't struggling to push his hands away. To his amazement, Kathy was the initiator, lowering her hands to places they had never been before.

For the first time Kathy's hands joined in the frantic unzipping and unbuttoning, and they were naked except for their underwear. As their foreplay increased, he could feel the pounding of her heartbeat against his chest. Their muffled moaning began growing louder when her velvety hand finally touched his private for a second breakthrough, and the sound of blaring trumpets rang in Sean's head. In that moment of heated passion, he reciprocated and placed his finger inside her forbidden fruit.

Suddenly, Kathy tensed and squiggled away. "Maybe we shouldn't," she slurred. I don't know. I'm so confused."

"Kathy, sweetheart," Sean whispered. "I love you. Two years of going steady—suffering the agonizing frustrations of controlling our sexual cravings in the midst of high-octane-stimulation—has taken its toll. We're adults now. It's okay, making love is not a sin."

Gripping Sean's shoulders, Kathy pulled him back on top of her. Sean felt her heart pound faster, her breathing growing louder. Dizzy from lust, and both drenched from the stifling heat of their bodies, she pushed his hands away and softly said, "I'm afraid, Sean. I mean I want to, it's just that, oh, I don't know. I've never touched a man's private. It's throbbing. I can feel it pulsing. Oh, Sean I want you so bad. But I can't. Oh God, it feels so good to hold it. It's so huge."

His hands caressing her breasts and suckling her rigid nipples, he raised his head and whispered, "There's nothing wrong with what we're doing. It's instinctual. It's time we surrender and enjoy our passion."

Kathy pulled Sean back on top of her and their panting began growing louder. Her body quivering, Kathy aggressively guided his penis slowly inside her and Sean was swept into euphoria as his heart palpitated wildly. In silence, except for heavy breathing, they slowly began thrusting their hips in rhythm. When her juices began flowing and the friction eased, their hips began undulating faster.

Sean had half expected that Kathy would lie like a corpse while he made all the moves. That wasn't the case, he quickly learned. Their hearts throbbing and their bodies pulsating in harmony to the pounding surf, the tempo of their hips quickened, thrusting faster and faster. Their erotic arousal rose to new heights with each crescendo until the sand beneath them began to tremor like an earthquake.

The sleeping bag thrashed wildly as their bodies convulsed in synchronized unison, both undergoing massive fibrillation. Sean was on the verge of having an orgasm when Kathy suddenly shoved him away and screamed, "No! Stop! You can't ejaculate inside me." She fought like a wildcat and squirmed away. "We can't do this."

Sean gasped and gulped a chest full of air. "You baffle me. What the hell's wrong with you? Are you crazy? This is pure torture. You've flipped your noodles. I'm outta here." He fought to unzip the sleeping bag.

"Please, Sean," she whimpered. "There's no need to leave. I just don't want to get knocked up and be nursing a baby while I'm in college."

"Damn! You sure are one hell of a teaser. I was almost . . ." he groaned. "You bitch."

"How dare you call me that," Kathy yelled and slapped him hard across the face.

Regretful for his words, Sean whimpered, "I'm sorry."

"Don't you ever call me that again," she said and began sobbing.

"I don't know what came over me. Hushabye, sweetheart, I can't stand it when you cry."

"It's my fault," Kathy whispered. "I drank too much and lost control."

"We both did. Look, I'm suffocating. I feel like withdrawing into a cocoon for calling you that. I need air. He poked his head out of the sleeping bag and gulped a mouthful of frigid air into his lungs. *From the broiler, she goes into an artic freeze. She bewilders me.*

Kathy sniffled louder and her body trembled as she poked her head out into the cold night air. "I feel terrible for slapping you."

"I deserved it for cussing at you like that."

"We can do it some more if you have a rubber," she said candidly.

"Really."

"Do you have a prophylactic?"

"Yeah, I've got a pocketful of them."

"That was great sex, but I was thinking if you wanted to, we could do the 69 first," she bluntly whispered in his ear.

"Wow, I never in my life thought I'd hear you say that."

"I scrubbed really good," she said.

He kissed her. "So did I."

Moments later their bodies jerked spastically and a tremendous surge rushed through Sean until they both erupted. They talked openly about sex for a while before Sean dug through his bag and brought out a condom.

"That was certainly a learning experience in the art of mutual reciprocation," said Kathy. "The pleasure I derived from getting you off had my body pulsating."

"I felt the same way," he said. "Man, you sure were quivering."

"And you went spastic," she said, "Receiving is good, but giving is so much better. You taste delicious."

"So do you," he said. "You really fired up my erogenous zone. I was in a tailspin. Wanna do it again?"

Nearly an hour later, Sean felt Kathy's body tremor for the fifth time as their pelvis' collided until she collapsed exhausted and he held her close to him, whispering sweet words to each other.

The night sky was clear with a full moon when they finished dressing and crawled out of the tent. They were breathing heavily when they stood up.

Looking innocently at Sean, her eyes fluttering, Kathy softly said, "I've never experienced anything like that. It felt so good having you inside me. We can do it anytime as long as you use a rubber."

Sean smiled sheepishly and kissed her. "I love you and I love this sex stuff. My head was spinning in a cyclone, like I was free-falling in a stream of a million shooting stars."

"Tonight has been the most precious night of my life. I will cherish it forever."

Hand in hand and radiating love, they strolled barefoot along the water's edge, staring at the crackling bonfire and talking about marriage and children. When the music stopped, they gathered their gear and joined their classmates, helping Sandy and his band lug the equipment back up the steep cliff as a crescent moon shined directly above them. Kids, toting plastic sacks of empty beer cans and bottles, were moping about, mumbling the word curfew.

Kathy remained dewy-eyed when they tiptoed up the steps under the porch light. At her door, she looked too florescent for Sean to tell her of his decision to hit the road for the summer with Sal and Arnie. He dreaded her reaction since making the plan a few weeks ago and hadn't found the courage to tell her.

"Today has been the best day of my entire life," said Kathy, taking a keychain from out of her purse. "I really loved having sex with you."

"You sure had a whole bunch of orgasms. Each time you did, I went bonkers."

"I loved the mutual gratification best."

After a long goodnight kiss, Sean promised to see her later that day. He told Kathy he had something important to tell her and she beamed as though she expected he might propose marriage. He felt a nervous twinge in the nape of his neck as he sauntered down the steps and over to his car.

Sean drove straight to Arnie's house to map out a route across the country. Arnie and Sal were standing on the sidewalk in the midst of a heated argument over who had the fastest car when Sean pulled up alongside of them and parked.

"Oh yeah," said Sal, "let's find out right now, tonight. Or are you chicken?"

"Okay, wise Guy," Arnie challenged. "You got your pink slip with you?"

"Come on you lamebrains, cut it out," Caroline pleaded impatiently from inside Arnie's car. "I've got to get home."

Arnie ignored her and grumbled at Sean, "What the heck's kept you so long?"

Sean grinned wildly. "Got waylaid at the junction."

"Cripes, man, you're always late. Hop in," Arnie said.

"That's okay. Think I'll ride with Sal. I want to be sitting in the winner's circle," Sean snickered and got into Sal's car. "You tell Mary Lou about the road trip?" Sean asked Sal.

"Yeah, she went totally whacko," said Sal, firing the engine and driving off. "She told me if I go not to bother calling her when I get back. She said it like she damn well meant it. I'm planning on talking to her in the morning after she cools down. How 'bout you, you tell Kathy?"

"Not yet," said Sean. "I'm like you. "I'm going to tell her tomorrow. But school's out pal. It's time to hit the road and seek out some adventure before tying the knot."

It was going on four in the morning when they dropped Caroline off at her house. On the drive back home, Sal swung his car across the center divide on Skyline Blvd., a deserted, two-lane road and came up fast alongside of Arnie's *FireEater*. The two cars were cruising evenly at about 75 mph when they both punched the gas. In a couple of seconds the needle of Sal's speedometer was bouncing around 120 mph. The initial G-force had Sean's head pushed back.

The two cars were dead even when Sean said, "Glad I decided to relinquish the crown of having the fastest car. It feels good to be relaxing in the passenger seat."

Sean's arm lay resting on the open window when he spotted a white Oldsmobile rolling on to the road with its headlights off in front of them. "Watch out Sal," Sean hollered.

In a blinding flash, Sal's car, traveling with the speedometer buried, spun around twice and careened off the car sideways. There was no time for Sean to brace for the impact and the passenger door got ripped off the hinges and Sean was hurled out of the car, bouncing along the gravelly shoulder of the road as Sal's *LoveMachine* flipped end over end. Sean finally skidded to a halt on the side of road.

His body in serious pain, Sean managed to sit up and study his hands and arms that were scraped raw. He heard a loud shout and saw two blurry, identical Arnies' running toward him. Sean reached up and felt his face and head. He studied his legs and thighs for traces of punctures or gashes and felt his teeth.

"Holy cow," Arnie bellowed. "Are you alright?"

Sean nodded, "I think so. Just a case of double vision."

"Come on. Sal's in deep trouble," said Arnie before he took off running to Sal's car.

Sean looked at where Sal's pink car lay topsy-turvy and then over at the Oldsmobile in the middle of the road. He got up and limped along as fast as he could.

Gas was spewing from the gas tank of Sal's car and Sal was muttering incoherently when Sean caught up to Arnie. They reached in through the window and helped pull Sal out. Just as they had dragged Sal a safe distance down the road, an enormous explosion erupted that rocked the ground. The three kids turned and watched Sal's pride and joy being engulfed in a blinding ball of flames. Sal sat with his knees to his chin staring at his burning car. He looked disoriented and didn't utter a word while Sean and Arnie examined him.

Appearing astonished, Arnie said, "I don't believe the two of you, you guys must be living charmed lives. It's a damn miracle you both survived."

Sean shook his head and helped Arnie raise Sal up. Muttering obscenities, Sal slowly revolved his bloody head and watched the flames shooting up from his car.

Sal's head had taken a good beating, but his limbs were all intact and he looked to be okay. Looking up at the eerie, black cloud mushrooming over Sal's smoldering car, Sal clasped his hands on his head and began gagging in tears. Moments later, Sal stared angrily at the white Oldsmobile in the middle of the road and ranted, "If anyone's inside that car, I'm kicking some ass." The three boys stared blankly at each other, each sensing the other's thoughts. The three boys clenched their fists and Sal and Arnie took off running to the Oldsmobile while Sean limped behind them.

Sean toddled over to the mangled car, wondering if there was someone inside. Arnie and Sal yanked the front doors open and stood with their fists cocked. In sickening revulsion, the three kids stared down at two of their graduating classmates, Tony Rizzoli and Wanda Skaggs, the high school homecoming queen. The wretched smell of puke flowed out of the car. They were sitting slumped forward, passed out with their heads lopsided and half naked. Slobbering vomit drooled from their chins, dripping onto their chests. Arnie cupped his ear and turned when they heard the faint whir of a siren and saw the flashing red lights coming from the south.

"Someone must have called the cops," said Arnie. "We'd better split the scene. We reek of booze."

Arnie and Sal slammed the doors.

"Call the police tomorrow and tell them that someone stopped and took you to a hospital," said Sean as they sprinted to Arnie's car.

"Better yet," said Arnie, call um and tell um your car was stolen."

Grimacing, the three kids turned and looked at Sal's car, reduced to molten metal before they got into Arnie's car and raced northward.

When they arrived back at Arnie's house, the three kids sat in the car popping open beer cans and passing a half pint of tequila around.

"Cripes, Sean," Arnie roared. "When I saw you bouncing down the highway like a ball of tumbleweed, I thought you were a goner for sure. Hell, at least maimed for life."

Sean belched. "It's a darn miracle I ain't dead."

Arnie swiped the hair from his eyes. "And then I see the *LoveMachine* flip over and I started thinking that the both of you were pushing up daisies." Arnie quaffed his beer can empty. "We should have kicked that asshole's butt on general principle. Passed out or not!"

"Naw," Sean chirped. "Those two are in the slammer by now. Once the cops caught a whiff of those two, I'm sure they nailed the suckers for drunk driving." He looked at Sal. "You've got insurance don't you?"

"You kidding, I had way too many speeding tickets. They dropped me."

"Yeah, me too," said Sean, nodding. "Between the speeding and excessive noise tickets, I must have gotten a dozen violations. Got lucky though, I lied through my teeth. Told the guy at the DMV it was just a passing phase I'd gone through. Told him I had matured and traded in the '57 for a four banger Volkswagen bug. The guy bought the crock of bull. Can you believe it? I still have my license."

Grinning, Sal raised his can of Bud and said, "I told um a similar story and they didn't yank my license either. Thanks for the tip, Sean."

"Glad it worked out for you."

Arnie gulped a swig of tequila and grimaced. "Dang, too bad about your car she was a real classic. Don't think I've ever seen another like it.

What about it, Sal, you coming along on the route 66 thing? Its going be a blast, a way to blow out the summer."

Sal's face tightened from taking a gulp. "Sounds great," he replied with a let down expression. "I wanna go, but now I've gotta save up some dough for a new set of wheels. It'd be dumb if I went."

"What do you mean you're not coming?" Sean said. "Ya gotta come."

"Yeah, Sal," said Arnie, "we're a threesome."

"Marylou had a conniption fit when I told her. Now I need to buy a car." Damn, that fries my ass." Sal looked quizzically at Arnie. "I can't believe Caroline didn't chew your butt out for taking off for the whole summer?"

Arnie took a swig. "Caroline knows who's in charge," he boasted. "You two sound like gutless, pussy-whipped pansies."

Sal and Sean tossed Arnie hostile glares.

"Just joking, guys," Arnie said, feigning an apology. "Why didn't you tell Kathy tonight?"

"I couldn't do it," said Sean, "everything was going so smoothly. I didn't want to end the night with a quarrel. But I'm going no matter what she says."

"I say we head south of the border," said Arnie. "Check out the beaches and the lovely senoritas."

"Yeah," said Sean, "I hear those Latin babes are hot and spicy, like red hot chili peppers. Come on Sal, ya gotta come."

"What am I supposed to do when we get back, hoof it and take buses to school? I ain't doing that. Those days are gone."

"We'll figure out something," said Arnie. "You guys are bashed and gashed pretty bad. Maybe I should take you both to the hospital and get you checked out."

Sean took a swallow. "Skip me but you'd better take Sal and have his head checked out. And get him some breath mints. And concoct a story."

"Amnesia," said Arnie. "I got it all worked out."

"Are you two nuts," said Sal. "I ain't going to the hospital the way I smell. They'd bust me for sure."

"Arnie's right," said Sean. "Wait a couple days until the alcohol is out of your system, and tell the cops you've been wandering around the city trying to figure out where you live and who you are."

"Now you're thinking," said Arnie.

They banged their beer cans and Arnie took Sal home.

The sun was rising over the eastern hills when Sean coasted into the driveway. Standing at the front door, he cussed aloud, realizing he had given his house key to his brother.

He searched for the spare key that was always buried in the flowerpot. It wasn't there and he checked under the mat and above the door. He searched the entire entry and couldn't find a key. He checked the garage door and the side door and grumbled profanities when he found them locked. He cussed some more when he couldn't budge any of the first floor windows open. Finding the house locked tight, he went to his car and grabbed a pry bar from out of the trunk.

He went into the backyard and pulled out a six foot ladder from a shed and leaned it against the side of the house below the roof overhang. He climbed up carrying a milk crate and pry bar. Carefully moving along the roof, he stopped at his bedroom window and cursed when it wouldn't open. He went to his sister's bedroom window and stood on the crate. The window easily jimmied open and he pulled himself up onto the sill. Taking great care not to make a peep, his body was three quarters inside when Heather let out a banshee cry.

Before Sean could utter a single word, Heather screamed louder and Sean plunged down on top of her. In a state of fear and panic, Heather flipped out, totally going ballistic in hysterics, slugging and kicking him.

"It's me," Sean shouted. "It's me, your brother, Sean."

But Heather's shrieks of, "Help" and "Rape" covered Sean's yells. In a rage, she continued to lash out wildly, pummeling him brutally with knee kicks and punches until their parent's barged through the door and flipped on the light switch. Sean's father stood at the doorway, wearing pajamas and slippers. His mother, in a state of glaring delirium, appeared to be suffering from a siege of distemper as she ranted.

Adjusting her nightgown, his mother, Rachel shouted, "What's going on here?"

"Nothing, Mom, everything's okay," said Sean.

"Why all this commotion and screaming?" Rachel yelled. Bleary-eyed and disheveled, Sean stammered to explain as he rolled off the bed and stood up. "I, uh, loaned Trevor my key this morning and the spare key in the flower pot wasn't there."

"My god, Sean," Heather said, regaining her composure and glaring at Sean. "You scared the life out of me. Heather rubbed her eyes and stared at Sean. "Dear Lord, have mercy, what happened to you? You're all cut up, a bloody mess."

Sean shrugged and said, "Nothing, just a little accident."

Rachel moved closer to Sean and ranted, "Little accident. Don't give me that mumbo jumbo. Coming home in the middle of the night all drenched in blood. My heavens, look at you, your clothes are ripped to shreds."

"Mom, I was at the beach party with Kathy. Sal had an accident on the way home. No big deal, nobody was hurt, just minor scrapes and bruises. There's no need for all this fuss."

Looking down at Sean's torn and bloody clothes, his father, Marty said, "Are you all right, Son?"

"Yes, Dad, I'm okay. They're just minor flesh wounds. Sal's car was totaled."

Rachel moved closer and studied Sean's knees. "Maybe you should get yourself checked out at the hospital. Those gashes could get infected." She went to examine his forehead and sniffed. Frowning and stepping backwards, she shouted, "Just as I suspected! You reek of a distillery."

With a look of distain, Marty asked, "Have you been drinking, son?"

Sean shrugged and said, "Yes, Dad, but only a couple beers."

"Are you sure you're okay, son?" Marty asked.

"Yes, Dad; I'm fine."

"Heed your Mother's advice and get to the hospital and have those gashes treated before they become infected," said Marty before he turned and walked out of the room.

Rachel grabbed Sean's hand. "Come with me, I'm driving you to the hospital."

"That's okay, Mother," said Heather, "I'll take him."

"Thank you, Heather. I've a busy day. I have to take your younger brothers to their soccer games early in the morning." Shaking her head, Rachel turned and left the room.

"There's no need for you to take me to the hospital, sis," said Sean.

Heather studied Sean's abrasions and gauges closely. "What do you mean, Sean, you look like you've been put through a meat grinder. These are severe lacerations. Mom and dad are right; they're ugly and could get infected. I'll get dressed and take you to the hospital."

Sean shrugged, touched by his Heather's concern. "Thanks for offering, sis, but that's not necessary. They're just minor cuts and scratches. I'll be okay."

"I insist on taking you to the hospital. That gash on your elbow needs stitches."

"That's okay, sis. Thanks, but I need to catch some shut-eye. It's been some kinda night. Just wrap me in iodine and gauze."

"Those things will leave scars," said Heather. "You don't want that, do you?"

"I'm young, sis, my body heals fast."

They argued for several minutes before Heather wrapped Sean in iodine and gauze. Sean conked out the instant his head rested on the pillow.

The house was empty when Sean awoke at ten in the morning and went to the bathroom. Gazing at his reflection in the mirror and looking like a mummy, he felt grateful to be alive. He ate a bowl of cereal, swallowed a glass of orange juice and quickly left for Arnie's house.

"When do you want to leave? Arnie asked Sean as the two kids sat on Arnie's bed after they had finished mapping out a route around the country.

"As soon as possible," said Sean. He took a deep breath. "Well, I'd better hustle over to Kathy's and get it over with."

"Good luck."

"Thanks, I'm gonna need all the luck I can get."

"How much money ya got?" Arnie asked.

"I got some hefty graduation gifts and plenty more's on the way from my uncle. He's loaded to the gills."

"Route 66," Arnie enthused, "here we come."

"I ain't looking forward to seeing Kathy," said Sean, "Something tells me that she ain't gonna take this lightly."

Sal busted through the door. "I'm going," he blurted. "Marylou wouldn't budge and give me any leeway. She threw my ring in the bushes and slammed the door in my face."

"Wow, that's heavy," said Arnie. "Give it some time, she'll come around and see it in a different light."

"Yeah, times a great healer," said Sean. "You call the police and tell em your car was stolen?"

Sal grinned. "Yeah, and I hit the Jack pot. My grandpa gave me two grand for a graduation present."

"Wow, that's a ton of dough," said Arnie.

"I earned it. I've been tuning his car since I turned thirteen. And I rebuilt his engine and dropped in a new tranny last summer."

"Welcome aboard, pal," said Sean. "Guess it's my turn to face the music. Wish me luck. See you cats later."

Halfway to Kathy's house, Sean started feeling antsy, worried about her reaction. Given the previous night's heated intimacy, the closer he came to her house the clammier his hands became.

Kathy displayed considerable compassion over Sean's injuries while they sat chatting on the porch about going to the beach. There was no way to avoid it any longer. Sean hoped for the remote possibility she might understand. But each time he went to tell her, she began rattling off all the plans she had made for them. He listened for a short while before he interrupted her and blurted, "I'm hitting the road with Arnie and Sal."

"What?" Kathy shouted, turning livid and jumping up, "For how long?"

"A couple three months."

"The whole summer," she yelled. "You're insane if you expect me to sit on my duff all summer while you're off romping across the country having the time of your life. You're the epitome of selfishness."

Sean stood up. "I expected you'd be upset, but not like this. Hey, lighten up, Kathy." A brainstorm came and he grinned, "I got an idea. Why don't you come with us? It's going to be a gas."

Glaring at Sean like he was a fool, Kathy gruffly said, "Are you kidding me, my father would kill me if I even dared to ask him."

"Tell him you're going with some girlfriends. He'll never know."

"Get serious," she yelled. "I'm leaving for college in August on my scholarship."

"I know, it's great and you deserve it. You're practically a straight A student."

Kathy looked glum. "I worked my fanny off to get it. You, you self-centered, egotistical bastard, what difference does it make? I'm never going to see you again. I've had it with you. You take off for the whole summer and you can forget this relationship."

She's bluffing. "Gee whiz, it's not like it's the end of the world. Hey, I love you, Kathy. You're my gal, forever and ever." He took her hand and pulled her close to him.

She appeared to soften. "I love you too, Sean, that's why I don't want you to go. It's not fair. What am I supposed to do? You expect me to sit here alone all summer twiddling my thumbs waiting for you; no way."

"Kathy, every guy yearns to head out and see some of the world when he comes of age. It's like a man's independence day, freedom, liberty and all that kind of stuff," he said, hoping she would understand.

"Why do you have to go this summer? Kathy pouted. "Why not next summer?"

"Look, sweetheart, I'm planning on dedicating the rest of my life to you. What's one measly summer?"

"It's supposed to be our summer together."

"The heck with Stanford," said Sean, I'll head back east with you and enroll at a college near you. Maybe I'll go to Michigan State and we can spend all our summers together forever."

She frowned. "That's all fine and dandy, but what about this summer? I feel like you're dumping me."

"That's ludicrous. Hey, angel eyes, I'm not dumping you. It's just that I . . ." Sean stopped and began suffering from guilt pangs as he watched Kathy's face turn flush and tiny tears trickled down her cheeks. Feeling morose, he thought back on the previous night, envisioning all their commitments. "Hey, come on, no weeping."

"How do you expect me to feel?" Kathy sniffled. "Last night you tell me all these sweet things and now you tell me you're taking off for the entire summer. Sometimes I don't think you have any feelings except for yourself and your car. I feel like giving you back your ring and breaking up."

Sean went into shock when Kathy started to undo her necklace. "Wait a minute, whoa, slow down. Let's not be rash. Okay, you've got my full attention. Can we compromise, how 'bout a month, maybe a little longer?"

"Two weeks would be better."

Sean shrugged. "Okay, two weeks. Now come on. Let's go to Santa Cruz and catch some waves and ride the roller coaster."

"You promise?"

"Of course."

10

ON A FOGGY morning three days after Sean told Kathy he would only be gone two weeks, he and his two buddies excitedly finished stuffing their gear into the trunk of Arnie's car. Restless for some hair-raising escapades, their surfboards strapped to the top, the three teens headed south on highway 101 to seek out thrills.

The temperature was hovering close to 105 degrees as they were highballing across the Mojave Desert on Route 66 the following afternoon.

Slouched in the front seat, flipping the pages of a *Playboy* magazine, Sean said, "She may not be a fuel-injected '57 Chevy, but *FireEater* ain't too shabby."

"Nice of you to say so," said Arnie, rolling a frosty can of root beer across his forehead. "She's running a little warm, but this baby's in sync." He took a gulp and burped.

The three kids, dressed in surfer clothes, wearing shades, and rubber flip-flops, were listening to Fats Domino singing *Blueberry Hill* coming from the radio. Sal was sprawled in the backseat with his head resting on a pillow, and his feet sticking out of the side window.

"Hey Sal," said Sean, scratching an itchy scab, "I love your new Corvette. That thing hauls ass."

Sal grinned. "It's a little cramped, but I'll get used to it once I've blown it out to 500 horsepower when we get back."

"That's gorilla horsepower," said Arnie. "Man, you're not planning on messing around."

"What else is there?" Sal said.

144

Sean turned around and held the centerfold in front of Sal's face, "Babes, dummy, chicks," he said, "Check out this hot bunny."

Sal grabbed the *Playboy* out of Sean's hands and licked his lips. "That's Jane Mansfield. Man, what a body she has."

Their adrenaline was pumping when the three chums arrived at the Grand Canyon and they spent a couple of day's white water rafting on the Colorado River.

Things really began to perk up when they ventured across the border into Juarez, Mexico. With no age restriction on drinking, they stopped at the first sleazy bar they came across. Talking in deep voices, the three boys swaggered over to the bar and ordered a round of tequila shots. The hefty bartender slammed the shot glasses on the bar and filled them to the brim. The boys grinned at each other, clanked their glasses and swallowed them empty. Grimacing, they ordered another around, washed them down with cold frothy beers and left to find a nights lodging.

After parking the car and checking into a motel with a heated pool, they staggered along Porfirio Diaz and stumbled into a strip joint. A couple of flat-topped Marines were standing at the bar within ear-range. The two uniformed soldiers were boasting of their sexual exploits at a local bordello. The kids were staring at the strippers dancing on the stage when they overheard one of the Marines describe the whorehouse. He said it was a palace with plush red carpets, clean rooms and hosted by a bevy of the world's most beautiful senoritas.

Taking their eyes off the strippers, the kids turned and faced the Marines and Arnie casually asked them, "Sorry for intruding but would you mind telling us where this palace is?"

The taller soldier took a swig and replied, "Not at all. It's just on the outskirts of town and cheap too."

The other shorter Marine reached inside his shirt pocket and said, "Here, take this card and you boys have yourselves a jolly good time."

The boys chatted with the Marines for a short while before they thanked them for the tip and hotfooted outside.

After hailing a taxi, in what seemed a flash, they were knocking on the carved, wooden doors of the Palace Bordello. A large woman, wearing a flimsy see-through nighty, greeted them. She escorted them to a dimly-lit, horseshoe-shaped bar and they sat on bar stools across from four elderly men. Ordering Margaritas, shots of tequila, they began glancing around for the bevy of beauties the Marines had bragged about.

"See anything that fancies you?" Arnie asked Sean.

"Not yet," Sean replied. "Think I'll hold off until I see something close to a ten."

"They got the part about this place being a palace right," said Sal, looking entranced. "This place is huge and wall to wall mirrors."

Sean looked at Sal and said, "You still dwelling over Marylou?"

Sal scratched his scalp and suddenly appeared sheepish. "Yeah, I guess so," he said. "I don't understand women."

"Who the heck does," said Sean, giving Sal a cocky grin. "So Sal, tell me, how many women have you had?"

"That's none of your darn business," Sal replied. "I've had my fair share of frolics."

"I mean the one's you've gone all the way with," said Sean.

"Would you back off," Sal angrily blurted.

"I'm not talking about making out or touchy feely," said Sean. "I'm talking about the babes you've done the deed with."

"I've had plenty. Well, I mean a few."

Sean leaned closer to Sal and said, "What's that mean?"

"Bug off, twerp."

Grinning at Arnie, Sean said, "Hey, Arnie, I think Sal's a virgin."

Sal shifted in his stool and glared at Sean. "I ain't no damn virgin," he gruffed.

"Whatever," said Arnie, snickering, "you won't be after tonight, right Sal?"

"You're darn tooting I'm getting laid," said Sal, "but she's gotta be a sexy fox. I ain't doing dog meat."

"Hey, Sal," said Sean, "I was only teasing."

The kids turned and began scanning the place. Sean's roving eyes widened when he spotted a young slender beauty step out from behind red velvet drapes.

Pointing, Sean said, "Hey, check out that slim babe."

Their eyes immediately locked onto the young girl, and Arnie wasted no time in flagging her to come over and join them. In the dim light, the raven-haired girl began to look prettier and prettier the closer she pranced sexily toward them. Standing at the bar, she looked to be an under-aged, frail schoolgirl the way she was fluttering her lashes and giggling. Sean sat breathless staring at her nutmeg colored breasts underneath a sheer silk blouse as she enticingly fanned her face. She had big, dark, innocent eyes and long, thick black eyelashes that were blinking in the REM mode. Her rigid nipples were dark and as lush as her ruby lips. The three kids flipped coins and Arnie and Sean grimaced when Sal won the toss.

"You lucky devil," said Sean.

Arnie motioned the girl toward Sal. "And I believe she has Spanish eyes for you," he said.

Sal flinched when the young girl sat on his lap and began unbuttoning his shirt.

The girl licked her lips, slid her hand on Sal's hairy chest and said, "You like come to my room?"

"This chick's high on drugs," said Sal.

Sean joined in the ribbing. "Who cares, Sal. Check out her seductive smile, and those ripe succulent boobs. Who gives a hoot if she's on drugs?"

"Yeah," Arnie added, "and those dark nipples are begging to be sucked. This sexy creature is lickable.

"It just doesn't feel right," said Sal.

"Get a grip, Sal," said Sean, "Marylou dumped you. This ain't like you're cheating."

"This tamale is definitely hot for your body," said Arnie.

"Yeah, Sal," said Sean, "the way she's licking her lips, she'll gobble the whole thing, I guarantee it."

Sal looked dubious and acted reluctant when the girl giggled and tweaked his cheek with her fingers. When she started to fondle him, Sal came alive.

"She's attractive and all," said Sal, "and my hormones are raging. What's troubling me is, the babe's a prostitute and she might have some contagious venereal disease, like syphilis or gonorrhea?"

"Don't let that bother you," said Arnie, "penicillin clears up that crap overnight. So quit copping out like a pathetic wimp, Sal. Don't dilly-dally, get with the program."

"Yeah, Sal," said Sean, "show this provocative lady your virility, your manhood. This ain't the time to be bashful. Be a man for Pete sake."

"Listen, you two," Sal squawked, "I ain't shy and I don't have to prove anything to you guys." Nervously, Sal gulped a shot of tequila.

Arnie ordered another round. Appearing hypnotized, Sal winced and fidgeted awkwardly as the young girl continued fondling him.

The girl stroked Sal's cheek and repeated, "You like come to my room?"

"I think those are the only words she knows in English," said Arnie.

Sean laughed and said, "She sure is horny. Come on Sal, she's begging you to nail her."

Sal turned furious. "I already told you two numbskulls, I ain't timid, and I'm no damn virgin. I just don't want to catch a disease."

"The women here are tested thoroughly every week by doctors," said one of the elderly men sitting across them.

"You boys have nothing to worry about," said another grey haired man. "The women in this place are clean and safe."

With some mild coaxing, encouragement, and the woman's risqué fondling, Sal slammed his glass on the bar. Transformed into Mister Macho, Sal rose from his chair, flexed his chest, and said in a fabricated deep voice, "Okay, come on honey. Let's you and I go do the deed and show these two lamebrains a thing or two."

"Thatta boy," said Arnie, "go slide your rod into that honey's moist love canal."

Sean and Arnie shook their heads and smiled at each other as they watched Sal saunter away with his hand on the senorita's butt until they disappeared behind the red velvet drapes.

Two senoritas were flaunting their stuff in front of Arnie and Sean as they watched Sal being led out from behind the red drapes by the young girl almost an hour later. Sal's legs were wobbly and his face was pale. He looked to be in a trance and on the verge of fainting as the girl held his arm and assisted him across the floor. Sal suddenly collapsed and dropped to his knees. The girl giggled and motioned for help. Arnie and Sean were laughing up a storm as they stumbled over and picked him up. Sal's eyes were blinking wildly as they carried him back to the bar and sat him on a stool while he was mumbling gibberish.

Staring seductively at Sean and Arnie, the girl giggled and said, "You like come to my room?"

Arnie and Sean wagged their heads and the girl left to sit on another fellow's lap.

"Come on, Sal," said Arnie, "tell us the nitty gritty. How hot was that lovely tamale?"

"Yeah, Sal," said Sean, "tell us the Scooby-do. Wha'd you two do?"

Sal didn't say a word. He just sat slumped on the stool, blinking his glassy eyes, looking to be in a state of vertigo. Several minutes passed before Sal returned to consciousness, a mass of sweaty flesh and began vividly recanting the steamy details.

Back at their motel room in the wee hours of the night and feeling groggy, the three kids were lying on their beds ready to turn in when Sal slurred, "How come you guys never did anything tonight?"

"Heck, Sal," said Sean, "Kathy and I have been going together for over two years. What do you think we do every Friday and Saturday night? Ya think we just hold hands and neck. Besides, I don't do dirty seconds."

"Sean's right," said Arnie, "she was the only decent babe in that place. The rest of the chicks in there were dog pooh. And I don't do dirty seconds either. Don't need to, Caroline and I have been getting it on for over a year. Face it Sal, you're just a late bloomer." Arnie grinned broadly. "Hey, did she really swallow it?"

Looking aflutter, his voice boastful, Sal nodded and said, "Yep, and after some seductive teasing, she slurped every drop like a suckling guppy. Then we screwed twice."

Arnie and Sean were staring at Sal with a hint of envy in their eyes when Arnie exploded a fart.

"Ah, man," bellowed Sean. "That was gross. Now the whole room's gonna stink."

Sal belched and farted. "It's the damn beans and spicy sauce."

"Then cut out eating that crap," said Sean.

"That's all there is to eat down here," said Sal as he let another one rip, "beans, chili peppers, and hot blooded Latin chicks."

A chain reaction of farts ensued.

The next day the three kids searched one bordello after the next, but none of the women came anywhere close to matching the previous night's youthful beauty. Arnie and Sean thought hard about returning to the Palace Bordello, but Sal already having had the girl; something didn't feel right.

*   *   *

Two and a half weeks passed since the boys set out on their journey when Sean began suffering guilt pangs for having told Kathy he'd only be gone two weeks. Sean had been calling her everyday since the day they left. Whenever he did get through, Carl repeatedly told Sean that Kathy was out. The last time Sean spoke to Carl, he told Carl that they had a major engine breakdown.

Arriving at the Gulf of Mexico and discovering how filthy the water was, the three kids turned grouchy, mostly from the unbearable humidity, stifling heat and loneliness. They were sitting in a smoke filled bar listening to Dixieland jazz when Sal huffed and grumbled, "I think I've had enough of this on the road stuff. I need to get back and patch things up with Marylou."

"Yeah," Arnie complained in a cranky voice, "nothing exciting is happening, at least not like the stuff on Route 66. To be honest with you guys, I'd rather be with Caroline than out here in this sweltering humidity, having to smell your stinky farts every night."

"Look who's talking," said Sean. "Anyway, you guys are right. I've been feeling guilty the past few days for having fibbed to Kathy about only being gone a couple weeks. I'm all for heading back. The water here sucks and I'm missing Kathy big time. I'm in the mood for some steamy romance."

"I could use a break from all your grumpiness these past few days," said Sal.

"Yeah, sure, Mister Stud Muffin," said Sean.

At midnight the next day, with the temperature flittering close to a sweltering 115 degrees, they arrived at the infernal city of Yuma, Arizona and pulled into a gas station. The only thing of interest came when the scraggly-toothed, pump-jockey told them, "Disss heed'll killsya ifin ya don has no arr condishner. Eh jizz gezz hodder an hodder da furdder wesss yalls driezz." The hillbilly was right; they entered hell a short while later. The heat got so bad that *FireEater's* engine was boiling over when they pulled into a rest stop. Arnie and Sal slept out under the stars in sleeping bags, while Sean lay sprawled across the back seat stripped down to his underpants and covered in sweat.

With both rear doors open, Sean awoke in the morning staring into the eyes of a huge scorpion. Its top-heavy pinchers were swaying and snapping as it crawled along the seat toward Sean's face. In a state of panic, screaming bloody murder, he smashed his head on the upper car door jamb before he squashed the scorpion with his fist and leapt out of the car. Morning traffic was zooming passed as Sean was jumping and swatting his underwear.

"What the hell, you gone cuckoo?" Arnie yelled as he and Sal sat up, staring at Sean.

"There was a damn scorpion in front of my face when I opened my eyes a minute ago," hollered Sean. "Honest, no bull, the damn thing spooked the living crap out of me."

"Then you'd best go wipe your butt," said Arnie.

Every hour or so, on the drive to Tijuana, Sal recounted the seamy details of his torrid encounter at the Palace Bordello in Mexico. Almost every night since the graduation party with Kathy in the sleeping bag, Sean woke up in the middle of a vivid Dream with his libido so aroused that sex was now an obsessive compulsion. When Arnie drove across the border into Tijuana, Mexico, Sean was beginning to feel anxious for one erotic exploit before making a life-long commitment on the day he would marry Kathy.

An unshaven bald man, with half his teeth missing and the other half rotting and black, stood lazily on a dirt-laden street corner. The man motioned for the boys to come over and mumbled, "Hey, gringos, you boys want good time? My daughter 15 and very tight pussy, only 5 Yankee dolla; you like. Mommy real nice too, big titties, you take both, only 10 dolla. Es a good deal."

Outraged, Sean grabbed the man's shirt collar, clenched a fist and shouted in the man's face, "You miserable slob; pimping your wife and daughter."

Arnie grabbed Sean's arm and pleaded, "No, don't hit the poor fool, he's just a beggar. The scumbag's not worth going to jail for."

"Come on let's get the hell out of Mexico," said Sal. "Hit some nice beaches, catch some waves and check out the Southern Californian, sun-worshipping deities."

Sean sneezed as he let go of the man's shirt and they walked away.

"It wrenched my stomach listening to that bastard peddle his 15 year old daughter and his wife too," said Sean. "Can you believe that? Let's scram out of this rat hole."

"I say we have a shot of tequila and a beer before we ride the big bombora," said Arnie.

"I second that motion," said Sal.

They stopped for a final shot of tequila and washed it down with cold beers. Coming out of the bar onto a crowded street the three teens were approached by a suave, short, slick-haired man. He was clean-shaven with an honest looking face, and dressed in a tailored suit, with shiny, wing-tip shoes.

The debonair man smiled and said, "Are you boys looking for a good time?"

The kids kept walking.

Following behind the boys, the man said, "You fellows will be sorry, upstairs are the finest women in all of Mexico."

Curious, the three teens stopped and turned to the man.

"Come, follow me," the man said. "You can see for yourselves."

In less than a minute, the man convinced the boys that just up a flight of stairs awaited the sexiest, and most erotic young women on the planet. The three kids looked at each other after hearing the man out. The temptation was so overwhelming they nodded their heads in agreement and were soon being led up a long flight of squeaky stairs. After glancing around at the inside of the dilapidated building and sniffing the brackish odor, they stopped and looked at each other.

"We're being conned," said Arnie.

"Yeah," said Sal, "this is bogus, let's boogie."

But the man told them to rest assured and guaranteed them that the finest, most exotic women in all of Mexico were just on the other side of the blue door he was pointing at. The man proceeded to lead the kids into a putrid smelling room filled with women in slinky clothing, seated on stained sofas, playing with rubber toys.

"You think that's a dildo?" Arnie asked.

"Don't know," replied Sean, "I've never seen one."

"Neither have I," said Sal, "but I know what that thing looks like and it's friggin' huge."

"There's not one good looking babe in here," said Arnie, "let's hit the road."

"My apologies," said the slick haired man as the boys turned and began walking out of the room.

Arnie cut him off, "Blow it out your ass."

"There has been a terrible mistake," said the man, following the boys out into the hallway. "The finer, classier and more beautiful women have been moved to the garden room because of the heat. There is a spa and it is air-conditioned. Please follow me. It is only across the way."

The three boys shook their heads in disgust.

Sean laughed at the smooth talker, feeling like a dumb-bell. "I think we've seen enough," he said.

The three boys were just about to descend the stairs when Sean's peripheral vision caught a glimpse of a tall, svelte beauty taking long strides down the hall. She was dressed in a silver studded, tight, black leather short skirt, with a taut, bare midriff and long tupelo honey legs. A matching black leather vest was unlaced up her front and she wore glossy, spiked black boots. The lean woman, oozing sex, quickly disappeared into a room and closed the door behind her.

"Hey, whoa, hold up, fellows," said Sean, pointing at the green door the woman had walked into. "Hey amigo, who was that babe?" Sean asked the man.

"Si, Senor," said the dapper man, grinning with eagerness. "I see you have exquisite taste buds. That is Ana Maria and she is indeed a very special woman. But she is also very expensive."

"What's expensive?" Sean asked.

The man's eyelids raised and said, "That, you must negotiate with the senorita."

Sean Squiggled his chin and said, "Man, that Amazon queen is some kind of wild-looking thing. You guys mind waiting while I take a closer gander?"

Arnie grinned. "Do your thing, man, we're in no hurry."

"I'm not saying anything's going to happen," said Sean. "I just want to take a peek close up. She sure looked hot."

"Take your time," said Sal. "We'll be having a beer at that cantina out front. And don't rush it."

"Sal's right," said Arnie, "that babe's got a dynamite bod. You'll be savoring the torrid encounter for years to come."

A moment later the man escorted Sean down the hall into a small, dank room that reminded Sean of a dungeon. The man politely asked Sean to wait while he went to fetch the senorita. Sean's hands began to perspire as he walked around the dimly lit room. He stopped to check out a stainless steel tray with assorted oils next to a massage table. He was examining a large replica of a silver bullet when he heard the door open and turned as the statuesque beauty strutted toward him. With piercing cat eyes, she stared at Sean as if she wanted to devour him. Sean stood mesmerized by her lewdness when she pulled apart her vest and exposed her firm breasts with rigid nipples that pointed upwards.

"What do you want to do big boy?" She asked in a sultry voice, taking a firm hold of Sean's collar.

"Uhhh, I don't know," he stuttered, staring at her breasts and smelling her musky scent. "The works," he blurted, "everything."

"The works, huh," her voice hardened, "B and D, S and M?"

Having heard or seen the abbreviations, Sean searched his mind for what they stood for. Unable to come up with anything, he said, "Look lady, "I'm not exactly sure what that means. But what the heck, sure, it sounds just fine to me."

The woman shifted her hips and ran her knee up Sean's inner thigh, pressing it tightly against his crotch and said, "Fifty Yankee greenbacks for one hour."

Staring at her breasts, he coughed and blurted, "Fifty dollars."

"You want the works, don't you?" Her voice was tough and raspy. She pulled him closer to her, lowered her hand, unzipped his pants and reached inside. Looking like she meant serious business, she began stroking his erection.

"Ahh," he squeaked, looking down at her taut midriff, "how 'bout twenty five for a half hour?"

"What could we accomplish in such a short amount of time; you want to enter the pleasure zone, don't you?"

"Ah, well, ah" he mumbled.

She pulled out her hand and twisted his cheek hard, dipped her fingers in a jar of goop, slid her hand back inside his pants and stroked him several times.

His mouth salivating, he said, "Okay, sure, 50 dollars." He was certain the wild eyed creature would teach him an erotic trick or two.

Sean took out his wallet, peeled out fifty bucks and handed it to her. She slipped the money into a small pocket, puckered her lips and grabbed a satin robe. "Take off your clothes, big boy," she said, handing him the robe. "I'll be back in a jiffy for some erogenous stimulation."

When she turned and strode out of the room, Sean began feeling guilty that he was about to cheat on Kathy. Stripped naked, he put on the bathrobe and sat on the massage table. Every conceivable fantasy he had ever imagined raced through his mind in vivid color. He saw the leather fetters hanging from the ceiling and then looked down at the iron shackles mounted on floor and shook his head. Seeing the steel manacles bolted to the walls, his body trembled and he remembered what the abbreviations stood for. *Bondage and discipline*, he thought. *Shit, this is a sado-masochistic torture chamber.* A wave of tingling vibrations pulsated through his spinal cord when Sean saw a leather-flogging whip and jumped off the table. *This is a bad omen*, he thought. *What the hell have you gotten yourself into? This is bizarre. This is creepy. You'd better get the hell out of here.* He quickly changed back into his clothes and sat nervously on the table, waiting to demand his money back. Five minutes passed, then ten, then twenty, until he realized he had been duped. He frantically burst through the door, charged down the hall and saw three burly thugs with surly expressions and unkempt greasy hair at the head of the stairs. They were slumped over the hand rail, looking mean as hell. He asked the men where the woman went and they nodded and shrugged their broad shoulders,

"No comprendo," said one of the ghoulish men.

Realizing it was a scam, Sean hollered, "I'll be back with my friends to kick your asses."

Sean bounded down the stairs. Out in the street, he saw Arnie and Sal drinking beers at an outside table. He ran over to them and explained what had happened.

"Calm down," gasped Arnie.

"The jerks were playing dumb," Sean said. "And that slut ripped me off for fifty big ones."

Arnie shoved his beer bottle away and stood up. "Then what the hell are we waiting for," he angrily said. "Let's go up there and kick their asses and get your money back."

"Whoa, Arnie, not so fast," cautioned Sean. "Those hombres are pretty tough looking."

"Who gives a damn," said Arnie. "Come on, we'll stomp their butts if they don't pony up the mullah. How many are there?"

"Three."

"Three against three," said Sal. "That makes it an even match."

"Guys, I'm tellin' ya, those dudes are big and mean. I'm thinking maybe it'd be wise if we get us some equalizers before we go up there."

Flared up and scowling, Arnie and Sal didn't bother listening and went storming up the stairs in a rage. Sal, a pint-sized runt, had his fists raised like a boxer. Sean shook his head and charged after them, thinking their added bravado had come from the tequila they had been drinking. Racing up the stairs behind Arnie and Sal, Sean saw the glint of a reflection from within a rolled-up magazine one of the thugs held.

"Hold up guys, Sean yelled. "They've got guns or knives."

Sean's warning came too late. The three goons pulled out chrome pipes. Sean heard the muffled bong of metal striking bone. Another conk followed and Sean felt the weight of Arnie and Sal's bodies plunging backwards against him as they plummeted down the stairs. The three thugs were merciless, clubbing and stomping them out in the street. Sean took a vicious blow to the back of the head and momentarily saw a plethora of stars. Dazed, the kids stumbled and fought for their lives, wildly slugging and kicking. It seemed the three thugs were intent on murdering them.

The battle was turning into a brutal massacre when a half dozen uniformed Navy sailors joined in the fracas and the tide swiftly shifted. The sailors fought with a fever and pounded the thugs until they lay bleeding face down in the dirty gutter. Rubbing their heads, the dazed graduates told the sailors what had happened. The sailors said they were frogmen and three of them arm-locked the thugs and dragged them up the stairs. As they waited, the kids bought the other three seamen a round of beer at the cantina.

"You soldiers saved our lives," Arnie told them. "Those goons would have killed us if you guys hadn't come along."

"Yeah, that's for sure," added Sal, "and all for a lousy fifty smackers."

"That's a lot of dinero south of the border," said one of sailors. "People get their throats slit for a lot less.

"You boys want some friendly advice," another sailor said, "steer clear of shoddy whorehouses like that."

"Hell, I know of a brothel about a mile from here," a flat topped redheaded sailor said. "Nice and clean and some mighty fine dames, cheap too."

Rubbing the knot on his head, Sean said, "I think I've had my fill of walking on the wild side."

"Me too," said Arnie. "A toast to the Navy and your heroics; God bless all of you."

Less than five minutes passed when the other three soldiers returned.

"Here's your fifty bucks," a grinning sailor said, handing Sean his money."

"Thanks, I really appreciate this."

"You three are beginning to look like cone-heads," a tall soldier said. "Best get some ice packs on your noggins. You boys took a good pounding. Pick up a jar of aspirin, they'll help lesson the pain."

A short while later, they all raised their beer glasses and guzzled heartily before the sailors bid the kids farewell. Taking their advice, the boys picked up a jar of aspirin, a couple sacks of ice and found a quiet motel with a night watchman. Arnie tipped the watchman an extra couple bucks and told him to keep a close eye on FireEater. They each popped a handful of aspirins and passed out with their heads burrowed in towels packed with ice.

Their heads were still aching when they awoke the next morning and Arnie grumbled, "Let's blow this Godforsaken hellhole and get our butts back to the good ole U. S. of A."

"I second that motion," said Sal.

"It's unanimous," Sean added. "Let's boogie outta this rat infested city."

The car loaded, they drove to the border crossing and waited in line. They sat watching the customs inspector rifle through the trunk of a car parked in front of them.

"Something's amiss," said Sean.

"I think I know what you're getting at," said Arnie. "That guy's not playing around. He's tearing that car apart."

"Ain't like Juarez," said Sal. "Those border patrol guys just smiled and waved us through."

"This sure as hell doesn't look like a warm welcome home greeting," said Sean.

The kids looked nervously at one another, displaying concern about the two cases of tequila, box of assorted liqueurs, cartons of firecrackers and cherry bombs that were stashed under their dirty laundry inside the trunk. They closely observed the border patrol officer rummaging through the bags and luggage inside the trunk.

Nervously tapping his fingers on the steering wheel, Arnie said, "What do you guys think? That dude looks to take his job seriously."

"Yeah," said Sean, "I've been watching him."

"Maybe we should turn around and dump the stuff," said Sal from the back seat.

"Maybe we're worrying over nothing," said Sean. That guy's not going to want to stick his hands in that mess and sift through all our stinky, poop-stained underwear. I highly doubt it. "Besides, it's only booze and firecrackers. It's not like we're dope smugglers."

When the car in front of them drove off, the border patrol officer ambled slowly over to Arnie's door and carefully studied the kids. "Looks like you boys had a rough night," said the man with a sour expression.

"We were jumped in an alleyway by a pack of ugly brutes," said Arnie. "But we got lucky. Some Navy frogmen saw what was happening and saved our butts."

"You boys were fortunate. Where you kids coming from?"

"Just Tijuana, Officer," Arnie replied, respectfully.

"Been in Mexico long?" the officer prodded, as his eyes roved around the inside of the car.

"Just overnight," Arnie casually said.

The officer suddenly glanced suspiciously over at Sean and Sal. "You young fellows have anything to declare?"

"No, sir," the three boys replied in unison.

The officer raised his glasses, turned and focused on Arnie. "Are you sure about that?"

"Ah, yes sir," Arnie responded hesitantly.

Stepping backwards, the officer said, "Then you won't mind opening the trunk so I may take a peek."

"Uh, sure thing, sir," Arnie said, opening the door and getting out.

After Arnie opened the trunk, Sean and Sal sat nervously watching in disbelief as the man's gloved hands began to ransack through the pile of dirty underwear. The man pulled out a bottle of tequila and held it up as his cold steel-gray eyes glared through the rear window.

Looking at Arnie with a stern expression, the officer asked, "Any of you boys twenty one?"

Arnie wagged his head and shrugged.

The officer pointed at a parking area in front of a building and told Arnie, "You mind pulling your car over to that inspection station. I'll need to see some identification, proof of insurance and vehicle registration."

Shortly later, the boys sat sullen-faced, sweating profusely inside an interrogation room. Dark visions of being garbed in a black-and-white striped prison outfit, working on a chain gang, with his leg shackled to a ball and chain as he crushed rocks with a sledgehammer, rankled through Sean's mind.

Almost an hour had past when another border patrol officer came back into the interrogation room carrying a thick black book. He looked each of kids square in the eyes one at a time and informed them in a harsh voice, "What you boys have done is tantamount to smuggling."

The boys cringed as the officer continued.

"Smuggling contraband is a serious crime with severe consequences and retributions. But since you kids have no criminal records and appear to be clean-cut, I've decided to bend the rules a little and save you from incarceration. However, you are each being penalized fifty-dollars and the contraband is to be confiscated. Can you boys pay the fine today?"

"Yes sir," they each rang out.

After paying their fines, the trio walked outside and shook their heads, staring at the seats, carpeting, headliner and their gear strewn on the pavement all around Arnie's car.

"Aw, crap, they totally gutted my car," said Arnie.

"Who cares," said Sal, "we're outta this place."

"Come on," said Sean, "it won't take us long to put everything back."

Arnie's car pieced back together, the kids were back in sunny California.

"If you hadn't hesitated and muttered, 'ah,' when that inspector asked if you had anything to declare, we'd have never gotten busted," Sean complained to Arnie.

"Yeah, Arnie, that was a dead giveaway," Sal huffed.

"Jump on my case, like it was all my dang fault, like you two never chipped in and bought any of that crap. And you, Sean, wipe that smug grin from your face. You told me the guy wouldn't sort through the underwear."

"How the heck was I to know he'd search through all that smelly stuff?"

Over the course of their leisurely drive north back to San Francisco, they drove along the coast and slept on sandy beaches. They caught a wave here and there and checked out the tanned Southern California deities. All Sean could think about, while being pelted by sea spray, was that hot night on the beach with Kathy. He wondered how upset she'd be at his being gone a little over three weeks instead of two. But he wasn't too worried, he thought he had done a good job in covering his tracks by having called Carl and giving him the perfect alibi. *With all these welts, bruises and knots on my head,* Sean thought, *she has to forgive me. It's clear evidence that we took a brutal bashing. She's got to believe me.*

"You're in for some good times at USC, Arnie," said Sean, peeling an orange, "the Southern California babes are buff and sure like to flaunt their stuff."

"Nude beaches too," said Arnie. "And teeny-boppers skinny dipping and hanging ten in the raw. How are the chicks at Stanford, Sean?"

"Not many around the day I went there," said Sean. "The few I saw looked too brainy and porky, wearing braces, thick glasses, with pencils wedged in their ears."

Sal laughed. "That's the way Marylou looked when I met her, slow in developing. Then one day she lost her baby flab and whammo, she transformed into a drop-dead knockout."

"You're a lucky guy. What's it like up at Santa Rosa JC?" Arnie asked Sal.

"I'm only going there for a semester," said Sal. "Then I'm transferring to Yale if they've accepted my application. Read an article that said the coeds are running around buck-ass naked at toga parties, bacchanals playing hide and seek with foxy Maenads."

"Wild sex orgies," said Sean, "now that's my kind of campus."

"I'm making it my minor," said Arnie.

"I'm thinking of changing my major from philosophy to aeronautics or jet propulsion," said Sal. "Now that the Russians have Sputnik orbiting, the Ruskies are watching everything we do. This country's gonna need help boosting the thrust power in our rockets if we want to stay in the moon race."

"You still planning on majoring in psychology?" Arnie asked Sean.

"Yeah, I kinda dig the deep stuff," said Sean, "But who knows."

*   *   *

Arriving home at midnight, Sean sacked out the minute he laid on the bed and pulled the blankets up to his neck. He woke up at noon and soaked in the bathtub, laboriously scrubbing away the grime. His adrenaline pumping with excitement over seeing Kathy, after he finished shaving, he sprinkled some drops of English Leather on his palm and patted his cheeks.

The engine blew and then we were robbed and beaten up," Sean thought on the drive to Kathy's house, *it's foolproof.*

Full of zealousness and whistling happily, he rounded the corner onto Kathy's block and saw a guy and a girl leaning against a Harley Davidson motorcycle parked in front of her house. Driving closer, he began thinking, *Naw, no way. She wouldn't. It can't be her.*

He rolled to a stop alongside of the motorcycle, only able to see the back of the girl with long blond hair and her arm wrapped around the guy. *It can't be, it's impossible, she wouldn't.* Sean's body shook when the guy turned and he saw the gloating face of Scott Simpson, leering at him with a whatcha gonna do about it expression. Sean's entire body convulsed when Kathy turned and stared at him, her eyes wide and her mouth gaping. Trembling, Sean blinked, closed his eyes, and shook his head, thinking he was having a bad nightmare. Suffering from an invasion of sudden traumatic shock, Sean opened his eyes.

"Get out of here you lying bastard," Kathy hollered. "Did you expect me to be waiting for you with open arms? Go on back to your friends. They're more important to you than me."

Realizing the impact of the repulsive truth he was witnessing, a knifing pain stabbed Sean's heart. The massive throb inside his skull felt as if his head was about to explode. The sudden compulsion Sean felt to burst out of his car and charge over and smash Scott Simpson's throat was overwhelming. Then Sean watched Kathy's father come storming down the steps.

The bitch, thought Sean. *The two-timing bitch, what a miserable traitor.*

Looking fiendish, Scott Simpson shoved Kathy away, pulled out a switchblade and charged Sean's car. "I'm gonna slash you to ribbons, you fucking prick."

Carl quickly swatted the knife out of Scott's hand and grabbed him in a headlock. "Get inside the house this instant, Kathy," Carl shouted at Kathy and turned and stared at Sean as Kathy ran into the house. "Get away from here," Carl yelled at Sean, "can't you see the damage you've caused."

In a flash, mumbling a slew cuss words, Sean revved the engine, popped the clutch and raced off. Swollen with tears, his heart strangled, he drove aimlessly around for hours. Choking and crying, he drove home. The house was empty when he ran inside the bathroom and stuck his head into the toilet. Finished throwing up, he charged into the garage, grabbed an ax from a shelf and drove to where he had carved their initials into the withering ancient oak tree. Wildly, he hacked away until not a trace remained of the heart and their initials. Laughing aloud and crying, he gagged and yelled, "The fucking dark angel couldn't wait one measly extra week." He looked upward at the sky, "What did I do to deserve this? What? What in hell did I do that was so terribly wrong? What?"

After a long tantrum, he drove to his father's school and waited inside his office.

"Hi, Dad," said Sean, rising from the chair when his father opened the door.

His father, Marty froze at the doorway with a concerned expression. "My God, what on earth happened to you, my son?" Marty said, hurriedly walking toward Sean. "You're all cut up and bruised," He closely studied Sean's face. "What's happened to you? Why are you crying?"

Sean spilled his guts out. When he finished, his father gave him a hug, patted him on his shoulder and said, "Life is not a straight line, my son."

"The low blow was that I found her with my arch nemesis," Sean blurted. "I hate that guy. If I had had a gun, I would have shot that no good louse."

"Killing is never the solution in attaining revival."

"I know," said Sean. "I never felt that way before. How could she be so cruel?"

Marty sat at his desk and began tapping a pencil on sheet music. "I don't have an answer," said Marty. "It's a riddle. Look son, you're a young and handsome boy. You'll find another woman."

"But I loved her, Dad," Sean blurted. "I wanted to marry her. I was only gone a little over three weeks, three lousy, measly weeks. Why couldn't she have waited?"

"I don't have the answer, it's puzzling, but consider yourself lucky. You wouldn't have wanted her for your bride. It's for the best, son. You'll meet plenty of fine ladies in college. Absorb yourself in expanding your mind. In time, your heart will mend. Time is the greatest healer of a broken heart.

"I just don't understand."

"There are many variations to love," said Marty. "The stronger bond comes with age and maturity."

"I read something about that in my psych class. Wasn't it Freud who said that?"

"Very good, son, he referred to adolescent love as idyllic infatuation and called it puppy love. Recuperating from shattered puppy love is much easier than recovering from truly deep love. This girl didn't love you. I know how you must feel; I've had my share of broken hearts when I was a teenager before I had the good fortune to meet your mother when I finished college. We have our disagreements but we always manage to resolve them. Imagine how you would feel if you had been married to that girl."

"You're right, Dad. I always learn something from you whenever we have our chats."

"That's what fathers are for. Aside from the battering you took in Mexico, how was your trip?"

Sean shook his head and said, "Boring. I'm thinking about hitch hiking around Europe next summer."

"Your Mother and I wanted to do that before your sister came around. Well, son, I have another class to teach. Drop by Bimbo's later tonight and we'll talk some more between sets."

"I will. Thanks for listening and steering me on a new course, Dad. Like always, you've been a great support."

A week later, Carolyn called Sean and set him up with a hot blind date. Three months after their first date, Sean and the blond bombshell, Christy Mc Vay were engaged to be married.

The End